CHRISTA WOLF

was born in Landsberg, Warthe in 1929. She studied German at Jena and Leipzig universities and has worked as an editor, lecturer, journalist and critic. She has written four novels: *Der Geteilte Himmel (The Divided Heaven,* 1963), *Nachdenken über Christa T. (The Quest for Christa T.,* 1968), *Kindheitsmuster (A Model Childhood,* 1977) and *Kein Ort, Nirgends (No Place on Earth,* 1979). She has also written short stories, essays and film scripts. Christa Wolf won the Heinrich Mann Prize in 1963, the National Prize of the DDR for Art and Literature in 1964, the Bremer Literature Prize in 1978, and the Georg-Büchner Prize in 1980.

Christa Wolf is a committed socialist of independent temper and for several years she was a member of the central committee of the East German Writers' Union. One of the most important writers to come out of Eastern Europe, Christa Wolf's writings reflect her preoccupation with the personal suppressions and official silences under Nazism, and with the events in Germany which followed the war.

In 1982 she was awarded a guest lectureship at the University of Frankfurt, where in May she gave a series of five 'Lectures on Poetics'. These related to studies and travels undertaken in Greece in 1980. The fifth 'lecture' was revised and expanded for publication as *C*

Virago also publishes *A Model C* and *Cassandra.* Christa Wolf's boo will be published by Virago in 198

VIRAGO
MODERN
CLASSIC

NUMBER
75

The Quest for Christa T

by Christa Wolf

Translated by Christopher Middleton

Virago

Published by VIRAGO PRESS Limited 1982
20-23 Mandela Street, Camden Town, London NW1, 0HQ

Reprinted 1985, 1988
The Quest for Christa T was originally published in German
under the title *Nachdenken über Christa T.,*
by Mitteldeutscher Verlag, Halle, 1968

English translation © Farrar, Straus and Giroux, Inc. 1970
Copyright © 1968 by Christa Wolf

Printed in Great Britain by litho
by Cox & Wyman Ltd., Reading, Berks.

British Library Cataloguing in Publication Data
Wolf, Christa
The quest for Christa T.—
(Virago modern classics)
I. Title   II. Nachdenken über Christa T. *English*
833'.914[F]   PT2685.036
ISBN 0-86068-221-8

This coming-to-oneself—what is it?

JOHANNES R. BECHER

Christa T. is a fictional character. Several of the quotations from diaries, sketches, and letters come from real-life sources.

I did not consider myself bound by fidelity to external details. The minor characters and the situations are invented: any resemblance between them and living persons or actual events is accidental.

C. W.

The Quest for Christa T

The quest for her: in the thought of her. And of *the attempt to be oneself*. She speaks of this in her diaries, which we have, on the loose manuscript pages that have been found, and between the lines of those letters of hers that are known to me. I must forget my memory of Christa T.— that is what these documents have taught me. Memory puts a deceptive color on things.

But must we give her up for lost?

I feel that she is disappearing. There she lies, in her village cemetery, beneath the two buckthorn bushes, dead among the dead. What is she doing there? Six feet of earth on top of her, and the Mecklenburg sky above, the larks calling in springtime, summer storms, the winds in autumn, and the snow. She's disappearing. No ears now to hear complaints with; no eyes to see tears with; no mouth with which to answer reproaches. The complaints, tears, and reproaches

3

are still with us, and they are useless. Finally we're shown the door, and we try to find consolation in the oblivion which people call memory.

Yet she still needs to be protected against oblivion. This is where the evasions begin. It's not against oblivion that she must be protected, but against being forgotten. For she, naturally, forgets; she has forgotten herself, us, heaven and earth, rain and snow. But I can still see her. Worse, I can do what I like with her. I can summon her up quite easily with a quotation, more than I could do for most living people. She moves, if I want her to. Effortlessly she walks before me, yes, that's her long stride, her shambling walk. And there too, proof enough, is the big red and white ball she's chasing on the beach. The voice I hear isn't the voice of a ghost: no doubt about it, it's her voice, it is Christa T. Invoking her, lulling my suspicions, I even name her name, and now I'm quite certain of her. But all the time I know that it's a film of shadows being run off the reel, a film that was once projected in the real light of cities, landscapes, living rooms. Suspicions, suspicions: what is this fear doing to me?

For the fear is something new. It's as if she had to die all over again, or as if I was failing an obligation to do something important. I'd never realized that, for a whole year, her image in my mind hasn't changed; and there's no hope of her changing. Not a person or thing in the world can make her dark fuzzy hair go gray as mine will. No new wrinkles will appear at the corners of her eyes. She was older than I, and now she's younger: thirty-five, terribly young.

Then I realize that this is what departure means. The thing keeps unwinding, with its assiduous whir, but there's nothing left to project: with a jerk the film's notched end jumps free, turns once more, and once more, then it brings the machine to a stop, hangs there, shifting a little in the slight breeze which is always blowing.

Fear, yes.

She really might have died, almost. But she mustn't leave us. This is the time at which to think more of her, to think her further, to let her live and grow older as other people do. It was negligent sorrow that made her almost disappear, imprecise memory, vague knowledge. Understandable enough. Left to herself, she was gone; that was always the way with her. At the last moment, one has the thought of working on her.

Under a sort of compulsion, to be sure. But who is being compelled? She herself? And to what end? To make her stay? —Let's put all the evasions behind us.

No: the compulsion to make her stand and be recognized.

Useless to pretend it's for her sake. Once and for all, she doesn't need us. So we should be certain of one thing: that it's for our sake. Because it seems that we need her.

In my last letter to her—I knew it was the last and I hadn't learned how to write last letters—all I could think of doing was to reproach her for wanting to leave, having to leave. But I did try to find a remedy for separation: I reminded her of the moment which I've always regarded as the beginning of our relationship. As our first meeting. I don't know if she noticed this moment, or whenever else it was that I came into her life. We never talked about it.

I

It was the day on which I saw her blowing a trumpet. She'd probably been in our class for several months. I knew her long limbs and shambling walk and the short artless pigtail held by a clasp, knew them by heart, and her dark voice too, which was rather husky, and her slight lisp.

I saw and heard all that for the first time on the first morning she appeared among us (for that was it: she simply appeared). She sat at the back of the class and didn't seem at all eager to get to know us. She never showed eagerness about anything. She sat on her bench at the back and looked at our teacher in just the same way: uneager, without eagerness, if that helps anyone to picture it. For her look wasn't hostile. Yet it may have seemed so, among the customarily yielding looks which our teacher expected of us. Our teacher lived by such looks, I've since come to think.

Well now, welcome among us, and what's our newcomer's name? She didn't stand up. She gave her name, in a rather husky voice, with a slight lisp: Christa T. Was it possible, had she frowned, just for an instant, when our teacher used the familiar form of address? Another minute and she'd have been put in her place.

Where are you from, newcomer? Ah, not from the Ruhr where they've had all the bombing? Not from blitzed Berlin? Eichholz—good heavens. Near Friedeberg. Zechow, Zantoch, Zanzin, Friedeberg—we thirty local children went mentally along the line of train stops. Piqued, of course. Here she comes creeping out of her village-schoolteacher father's house, hardly thirty miles from here, and gives us this kind of look. If she had a few dozen smoking foundry chimneys behind her, or at least the Schlesischer Bahnhof and the Kurfürstendamm . . . But pine trees and gorse bushes and heather, the same summer smell we'd had enough of to last a lifetime, the broad cheekbones and brownish skin, and behaving like this?

What was one supposed to think?

Nothing. I thought nothing at all of it, but gazed out of the window, bored, so that anyone could see, if they wanted to know. I could see the gym teacher with the marker pennons marking out her everlasting ball-game field; it was more pleasing to look at that than at the way this newcomer treated our teacher. The way she kept the reins on her, turning the interrogation, which would have been statutory, into a conversation, and how she even decided what the class was to talk about. I couldn't believe my ears: the topic she suggested was "The Forest." The whistle was blowing for the start of the ball game, but I turned my head and stared at the newcomer, who had declined to name a favorite school topic because her favorite activity was walking in the woods. So that was how the teacher's voice sounded when she was giving in: wasn't it the limit?

The air was thick with betrayal. But who was the traitor, who was being betrayed?

Well now, the class must give our newcomer, Christa T.,

7

the friend of the forest, a nice warm friendly welcome, as it always does.

I drew down the corners of my mouth: not me. No friendly welcome from me. I won't give her anything. Ignore her.

Difficult to say, all the same, why people brought me information about the newcomer. So what? I said, at the end of every statement. But I did first listen to what they said. That she was one year older than we were, for she came from a secondary school and had to repeat a year. That she was living *en pension* in the town and only went home at weekends. So what? That her family called her Krischan. Krischan? Looks just like her: Krischan.

And that was what I mostly called her.

She didn't go out of her way to find a welcome, friendly or unfriendly. She wasn't interested in being accepted. We didn't interest her "excessively"—that word was just going the rounds. She's not excessively polite, is she? I looked up in the air and said: So what?

Thinks rather a lot of herself, this new girl. She's crazy.

The truth was: she didn't need us. She came and she went; that was all that could be said about her.

It was I who ended up knowing most about her. And if not the most, then enough. Which is how it turned out.

The air-raid alerts grew longer, the draft calls gloomier and feebler, we didn't notice anything and then November had come again. Anyway it was a gray day, so probably it was in November. A month without any sense whatever, and no sense was coming our way either. We were walking through the town in small groups, the all-clear had taken us by surprise: it was too late to go back to school and too early to go home. We hadn't been given any homework for months, and the sun wasn't shining either. What was there for us to do, anyway, among all the soldiers and war widows and antiaircraft auxiliaries? And what could we do even in the park: the deer meadow was fenced off as ever,

8

but there were no deer, and we weren't allowed to skate there any more.

Who had told us so? Nobody. Why were we looking at one another in that curious way?

No reason. If you don't get a good night's sleep, you see ghosts, or hear them.

There was the afternoon showing of the film *The Golden City*, but as usual it wasn't open to young people. One had to ask Sybille to put her hair up and dress in her mother's high-heeled shoes, put lipstick on her lips, red as they were without it, make herself look just about eighteen, so that we could all get past the usherette behind her. Sybille wanted good words from us, and we gave them, we danced attendance upon her; but as for Christa T., who was with us, because she might as well be there as anywhere else, nobody paid the least attention to her.

Then she began to blow, or to shout, there's no proper word for it. It was this I reminded her of, or wanted to, in my last letter, but she wasn't reading any more letters, she was dying. She was always tall, and thin, until the last years, after she'd had the children. So there she was, walking along in front, stalking head-in-air along the curb, and suddenly she put a rolled newspaper to her mouth and let go with her shout: HOOOHAAHOOO—something like that. She blew her trumpet and the off-duty sergeants and corporals of the local defense corps stopped and stared and shook their heads at her. Well, she's cuckoo, that's for sure. Now you see what she can be like, one of the other girls said to me.

Yes, I saw it. I grinned like all the others, but knew that I shouldn't. For me, unlike the others, it wasn't the first scene of this kind. I tried to recall a previous occasion when she could have walked on ahead of me, yet found there wasn't one. I'd simply known it. Not that I'd have expected the trumpet, that would have been lying. But, as everyone knows, you can't see what you don't know, and I was seeing her. I can see her now, today, but it's only today that I can see her aright. And can tell better how long it takes and what it costs to wipe this silly grin off one's face; I can smile at my old impatience. Never, never again did I want to stand outside the town park, outside the fenced-in deer meadow, on a day without any sunshine—and it was another person who'd let go with that shout which erased everything and for a fraction of a second lifted the sky up higher. I could feel it falling back again on my shoulders.

How can she be induced to turn around and notice me? That was the question. Friedeberg. Yes, I was interested in the country around Friedeberg. And in a village called Eichholz. In a village schoolmaster's house, with a low-hung mossy roof . . . I know it all no better now than I did in those days. If we did go on excursions we hardly got beyond Beyersdorf and Altensorge, though twice we traveled the two hours to Berlin, the Zoo station. The palace was still intact in those days; then we gave up, it was too far, and who'd have the heart to go there in wartime anyhow? Christa T. went there all the same in the summer of 1944, with a girlfriend, of whom I was jealous, who played Beethoven to her in the music room of her empty Berlin apartment by candlelight until the air-raid alert sounded. Then they blew out the candles and stood at the window. No, one couldn't approve of her way of risking things so far, a disaster, a death, a friendship. And the palace by that time couldn't be seen any more, only perhaps the wreckage, the green copper roof. More than that I can't remember.

I won't pretend that I remember things she talked about at that time. Only that the forests in the country around Friedeberg must be darker than forests elsewhere; and that there were more birds in them, obviously. Or that there were more birds if you knew all their names. That sort of thing. But that's about all.

She told me things when I expressly asked her, but I've forgotten them. Only after her death did she give an answer.

Her writings have taught me, more thoroughly than I ever could have expected, about the certainties and uncertainties of her childhood. Also that it cannot be hurtful to achieve certainty, once and for all, about some things, perhaps the most important things, while one is still a child. So that, when one leaves the land of childhood, seventeen years old perhaps, one has seen much and seen it for keeps. One must bargain on that, if one has only twice that long to live.

Not a word about this to me.

But some things she did tell me. She gave information; anyone could see who was asking the questions and who was answering them. We aroused envy, we were considered taboo, even before we exchanged a single word in confidence. Rapidly and regardlessly I had broken all other threads; suddenly I felt, with a sense of terror, that you'll come to a bad end if you suppress all the shouts prematurely; I had no time to lose. I wanted to share in a life that produced such shouts as her *hooohaahooo,* about which she must have knowledge. I saw her going around with others and talking in a friendly way with them, just as she went around and talked with me. I felt the valuable weeks slipping through my fingers, felt my weakness growing, had to force things, did everything the wrong way. I asked her—only today do I realize how clumsy I was being—who on earth can have put the flowers on Metz's desk, Metz of all people (our mathematics teacher). How should I know, she answered, calmly, and she was lying. We all agreed that Metz was macabre, truly so, that was our word for her. No point in arguing, but who'd put flowers on the desk of someone like that? Now I know that it was Christa T. and that she lied to me, because she saw no reason why she should tell me. Metz, Christa wrote later in her diary, was the only person in the school who didn't make her feel unfree and unhappy. —How foolish to feel hurt by that, after all this time.

I ignored the go-betweens; why didn't they notice that they came too late with all their gossip? I didn't hesitate to look across in her direction, to find out if she had noticed. She'd understood, she replied with a dark mocking look, which meant that she didn't regard this as a reason to come dancing out into the open. She was leaning against the railing of the gallery where we changed our clothes, and was looking down into the gym below, at the slogan on the opposite wall: FRISCH—FROMM—FROH—FREI. She put on her white blouse, tied the black triangular neckcloth, and pushed the leather toggle up, as we were all doing, for there had been an attempt on the Führer's life and we were wearing our uniforms to show our unswerving loyalty to him. I now thought that I knew her, I'd even called her on the telephone, and she'd answered calmly, but what she was thinking or seeing just now I didn't know. It burned me up, my powerlessness to explain to her why I had to know, whatever the cost.

I began to offer openings. Once our teacher had just walked past, replied to our salutation in her ringing tones and at the same time measured us from head to foot, so that, as usual, you felt there could be something wrong with how you looked; and I managed to ask: Don't you like her? Now it was clear who was betraying whom and why. Christa T. looked around and we were now both looking at our teacher. Her walk wasn't a stride any more but a self-righteous strut, and her stockings, darned all the way up the calf, were ugly and clumsily darned stockings, not the proud sacrifice of a German woman in the war's fifth year amid a textiles shortage. I looked at Christa T., astonished, as if she was the one to deliver the verdict. She's calculating, said Christa T., and her tone was simply factual. —I'd have preferred not to hear it, but I felt that she saw things as they were. She was right. She came from God knows where—since anyone can say Eichholz—ran around in the square schoolyard just as we did, though her choreography seemed to differ from ours in a way you could hardly define, walked down our few streets, all of them ending at the marketplace, sat down on the rim of the fountain, which bore our teacher's name (for our teacher came from one of the most influential families in the town), held her hand under the water, and looked about her with her usual thorough gaze. And suddenly it occurred to me that the water here was not, after all, the water of life itself, and the Marienkirche wasn't the world's sublimest building, and our town wasn't the only town in the world.

She wasn't aware of the effect she had, I know. I've seen her later, walking through other towns, with the same stride, the same amazed look in her eyes. It always seemed that she'd taken it upon herself to be at home everywhere and a stranger everywhere, at home and a stranger in the same instant; and as if from time to time it dawned on her what she was paying for and with.

Meanwhile, she gave some proofs that she wasn't averse to becoming dependent, as long as she herself could do the choosing. Openly, mockingly, and full of self-irony she told me, in token of her confidence, about the war-wounded teacher who had come to work as her father's assistant. How he played the organ, she said; and I had to imagine her sitting in the church aisle on Saturday afternoons while he played for her; it was most unlikely that she'd have gone to the Sunday service on his account. She watched my clumsy thoughts and smiled even more when I could find nothing to answer with, uneasy and foolish as my feelings were, since she must be ahead of me in "those things" too, I realized, and she must think me childish. Eventually I came up with "You'd better watch out!", as if I understood something, though not much, of matters known to her from closer experience. We were leaning against the school wall, which pressed down upon our shoulders; our book bags were on the ground beside us, and with the points of our shoes we were tracing circles in the gravel. Krischan, I said, not looking at her, Krischan you'll write, won't you? —The Christmas holidays were beginning.

Why not? she said. We'll see. Perhaps.

A thin cold snow began to fall. We'd stood there longer

13

than our talk lasted, and if I could paint I'd put that long wall down here and the two of us, very small, leaning against it, and behind us the big new square Hermann Goering School, red stone, lightly veiled by the gentle fall of snow. I wouldn't have to describe the cold light; the picture would in any case radiate the uneasiness I was feeling, because the dull and empty sky above us would be there for all to see; and that would be sure to have consequences, whether we liked it or not. Also one would be able to guess, from the picture, that under such a sky people can easily lose one another. And that we would soon be doing just that: losing one another and ourselves. The ingenuous open heart preserves one's ability to say "I" to a stranger, until a moment comes when this strange "I" returns and enters into "me" again. Then at one blow the heart is captive, one is prepossessed; that much can be foretold. Perhaps all our going out and coming in teaches us to repeat this moment. Perhaps it makes sense that Christa T., Krischan, should now be repeating it again.

The snow fell more thickly and a wind was blowing. We went our separate ways. I wrote her a letter, for she had her seventeenth birthday during these holidays. I openly offered her my friendship. I waited only for her answer, while my town, which would have to stay put if it were ever to mean the same to me, was being raised up high by the waves of refugees and retreating armies, like a ship being dashed relentlessly along. I saw all the commotion and didn't know what I was seeing. I was waiting for a letter. It arrived after New Year's Day, with the last postal truck from the east, and I carried it around with me for a long time afterward, many miles, until I lost it, naturally, like everything else. At least I had this pledge, although strictly speaking it contained no promises, no assurance, only a few quite friendly words and a groping tentative report on this young teacher. I never met him, and he never came up in our conversation; I even doubt now that he ever existed. But in those days it gave me hope, her talking about him.

All through January, while the place names shouted by the passing refugees became more and more familiar, my hope was more real than the identical faces of the people as they went by. Until one day a tired voice from the convoy shouted "Friedeberg." Suddenly hope was a thing of the past. I was just one of the other people. I tried imitating the expression on their faces; we still had five days. Then one day; then no time at all. Then I became one of them and in a few hours I'd forgotten that one can look from solid houses with horror and pity at people trekking by.

I didn't forget Christa T. I was sorry about her, as one is sorry about a promise that is unrepeatable and unfulfilled. That was why I gave her up for lost, with a single painful jolt, lost like everything else that was left behind. "Don't turn around, *dreh dich nicht um,* don't turn around, if anyone turns around or laughs . . ."

But we didn't laugh, heavens no. Rather we flung ourselves into the nearest ditch and wept; that was at least something. The story of our laughter, lost but found again years later, is quite another story.

2

Or not. Curious, how all the stories from that time relate, of their own accord, to her, to Christa T. Who'd have thought it, during her lifetime? Or does one just have to insist that her lifetime continues into the present, in order to relate to everything that becomes story, or history, or remains formless, material only.

She was, one could only suppose, extremely averse to anything formless. That's how she's to be recognized, if at all. When everything depended on one's getting away with a little light luggage, she kept a small book with her, which has now come into my hands, only loose pages by now, bound in blue flowered silk, and on the cover in her childish scrawl: *I would like to write poems and I like stories too.*

Ten years old, her factual tone. Write poems, "dichten," *condensare,* make dense, tighten; language helps. What did she want to make tight, and against what did it have to be resistant? Did she need that, among all her certainties? In her solid household, her village, over which the local boys launched a glider on whose wings they'd painted her name in great black letters? Among the dark forests, pine trees, what's more, tall ones as everywhere in our region, or in what is called "the bush." The sky more serene, the fine-weather clouds whiter than anywhere else: that too we can place among the certainties. And Erwin, of course, the blacksmith's son, who gave her the cast-iron ring that's hidden in a secret panel in her diary—which he needn't know about. Just as one couldn't guess that her grandfather, who tells unrivaled tales about hunting lions, has never been in Africa; but for a man who understands bees as he does— anything could be possible for him.

"A Canadian ignorant of Europe's hypocritical manners," that was his favorite line of verse; and it shows what sort of man he was. The opposite of her father, the village school-teacher T., who does oil paintings and investigates the history of the village in old church documents, to the displeasure of the cavalry captain who owns the big estate and isn't going to sit and watch while the schoolteacher in his writings belittles the family; the schoolteacher, this sickly man, unfit for military service, though he sends his younger daughter, a tomboy with a boy's name, to pick mushrooms in the estate's forests with a gang of village lads, without a permit of course, and they raid the apple trees in the orchard, so that the warden has to punish the lot of them by making them pick up stones off the captain's plowland.

Sternkind—kein Herrnkind: who can have said that? Later she wrote it down: Child of a star, not a great gentleman's child. Without comment. She wrote it down among the certainties. She knew: it was true. But it wouldn't have been right to waste any words on it.

Her fear of the warden is irrefutable; silently she admits she's not a gentleman's child. To stand, obscure among other obscurities, while the fires are blazing. The black-red-and-gold flags are being burned, one is five years old, and one's sister, not much older, comes in with a deathly pale face bringing someone into the house, one goes along and sees, and expects the worst, but all that happens is that the living-room windows are smashed, there's a draft, nobody has put the light on, suddenly it's dangerous to do so. One wants most to tell the grownups that anyone who's plucked up enough courage to smash windows somewhere would have taken to his heels as quickly as he could. But one hears that it was the milkman from the captain's estate, an adult, and he's said to have shouted "Socialist swine!" and not run away because his new uniform made him feel brave.

So one remembers the burning flags, not because of the flames, for things burn quickly and easily enough in the village, but because of the faces. Then she's standing, aged fifteen, among the others again, this time at the gateway to the park, and the fires are torches and in their flickering light the festively clad occupants of the estate walk with their guests from beneath the portal, and the brand-new Knight of the Iron Cross is among them. Then one's glad to be in the second row, obscure among other obscurities, so that the young Knight Lieutenant can't recognize anybody, even if he wanted to. But how should he still want to? How should he still turn to face Krischan, Krischan in her shorts and wind jacket, Krischan the only girl in the gang of boys, Krischan who walks up proudly to the other long-haired ones and says: Spoilsports can't play! Krischan with her death-leaps off the roof onto the barrel, Krischan as an old Turk at the fancy-dress ball, Krischan who goes out flushing the game for the hunt, who rolls through the village on her little wagon, rolls slap into the middle of the film team doing a take of *That Was My Life,* slap into the middle because the brakes don't work, just as Raddatz is taking careful aim to get an apple from a tree; and the boy up in the tree, up among the top branches with his cap full of apples, you can't see him; but it was Jochen, the young

Herr Lieutenant, Knight of the Iron Cross, and he fell out of the tree laughing.

Sternkind. Which doesn't necessarily mean a lucky child, Sunday's child. Not every star shines brightly and persistently. One has heard of difficult stars, with a changing light, disappearing, returning, not always visible. But that's not the point either. And what would it be then?

In January 1945 she traveled west with the last vehicles to get away, in the small cabin of a munitions truck. Worse than actual events was the fact that not even the horror itself could surprise one now. Nothing new under this sun, only the end, as long as it lasts. And the certainty: that it had to come. That's what a village inn must look like when mankind conspires to crowd into it, everyone, because of an unknowing fear. Pale-faced women, exhausted children, and soldiers about their daily business of moving away and on. The weariness that doesn't only come from six nights without sleep; the most important thing slips through one's fingers, and one doesn't even notice it. It is crouching on the floor; lucky if you've got a bit of wall to lean against. Christa T., to ward off despair, pulls a child to her lap. Then the radio overhead begins to roar: once more, even in hell itself, this fanatical overplayed voice, loyalty, loyalty to the Führer, even unto death. But she, Christa T., even before she's understood the man, feels herself going cold. Her body, as usual, has understood before her brain has, and the brain now has the heavy task of catching up, working up the terror that's in her limbs. So that is what it was all about, and this is how it must end. There's a curse on the people sitting here and on me as well. Except that she can't stand up any more when the song comes: there it is. I'm staying here. I'll hug this child. What's your name? Anneliese, a pretty name . . . *Über alles in der Welt* . . . I'm not going to raise my arm any more. I have the child, small warm breath. I won't sing the song with them any more. How they sing, the girls sitting along the bar; and even the soldiers, who were smoking and cursing as they leaned against the wall, stand up stiffly, pulled up straight by the song. Oh, your straight backs. How shall we ever stand up straight again?

The co-driver shouted, Let's go; they had the truck ready again. Christa T. jumped up into the cabin and squeezed in beside him, and now the night really began, and the snowstorm. Even before they reached the second village along the road they were stuck, it was no use shoveling, they had to get help. You'd better stay here, miss. She didn't say anything; everything that was happening to her fitted the nightmare exactly. Now she had crossed forever into the other world, the dark one, which had never been unknown to her—why else her inclination to "write poems," to tighten the structures, make resistant the beautiful, bright, and firm world that should be for her? Press your hands, both hands, against the rifts through which it keeps pouring, cold and dark . . .

Pity for the child I am, behind thick walls I hide, pity for the child I am, and the cold wind blows outside . . . Ten years old she'd been, shut out from other people's company because of insolence, and there it is, in her book, with the flowered silk covers. There she discovers consolation: in the lines she writes. One doesn't forget the wonderment any more, or the relief.

She wakes up in the night, the farmer and his wife are still there, they've been drinking and the phonograph is playing. I'll dance with you into the skies above. And they dance, too; behind the glass door their shadows are moving, suddenly they freeze. A screech. The farmer's wife has stepped on the tomcat, our good black tomcat, he's gentle and old, but he's hissing at the farmer's wife now, she lets out a screech; then silence. Worried, you run to the window, the moon is shining, then the farmer comes out with the tomcat, has grabbed him, cursing and swearing, as he flings him against the stable wall. Now you know how it sounds when bones crack, when something alive a moment ago drops to the ground. And now, overlavishly, for the farmer is a hot-tempered man, but to make a thorough job of it, now comes the roof tile. You take a step back, even stop your sister from going to the window, aren't surprised when she, the elder one, for the first time obeys you, almost as if she was afraid. She never did discover where the cat went. Much better if a mad dog had attacked him, not a mad man; if he'd died alone, how much better than having Father watch.

That's what happens when you're not being attentive.

Then you are seized by suspicions about broad daylight and the smooth faces. But at night the tomcat crouches on your chest, the great heavy beast, so that you're forced to get up and wander around, going to the maid's bed, Annemarie's, to demand with threats that she make room, which she does, trembling all over with fear. But when you wake up next morning in a strange bed, you've forgotten the night; which is more troubling, it really is, than anything else.

It wasn't Annemarie but another maid, it must have been, a later one, who suddenly went "crackers"—what cracked her?—and began to stare into the mirror, to be not all there, desperate and strange, so that you remembered again all the strangenesses you had known since earliest childhood. In fact, ever since the evening you stopped calling yourself by your name, Krischan, as everyone else did: though you tried this again more than twenty years later in the sketches I discovered: Krischan went, Krischan came . . . The "Child in the Evening" doesn't go and doesn't come. That poem is about being alone with one's misery and enduring it, for the first time refusing to let it be blown away. You don't know why this is so, but it is. Yesterday you'd still have gone to the kitchen, where your sister is helping your mother make the soup for the evening meal, alone, as she asked. But to-day, instead, you must go to the gate, holding to the slats, and must watch the gypsies leaving the village, and Anton and his wife and four children, farm workers from Mühlweg, have joined them. Once more you can't do now what you'd have done yesterday, shout "Kalle!" and wave. Hold up the flintstone that he gave me, only last week, as a goodbye present. But the only person looking at the child who stayed behind is the gypsy boy; did he make a face at her? He's free to do as he pleases. This morning he pulled his pants down in the street and left a heap right in front of the burgomaster's office; now it's his pleasure to despise everyone staying behind in the village, me included. The misery can get even worse. "I," the child thinks, "I" am different. Now the green gypsy wagon has disappeared into the darkness, nothing's left but an overturned handcart. Longing, a little fear, misery, and something like a birth. Durable enough to be fetched out and written down thirty years later. How else should I know of it?

Lucky for you, miss. The banal voice of life itself, the staunch co-driver holding the fistful of snow with which he'd rubbed her face. He'd had a sort of a feeling that she'd fall asleep, but it takes a good three hours to find a tractor for a tow on a night like this. She wants to laugh, Christa T., she can't take it seriously. A moment ago where was she, warm and hidden? It wouldn't be so bad to go back there. But the co-driver shakes her hard by the shoulder, jumps down and tells her to take a look. He shines his flashlight on a small, snow-covered bundle just beside the truck. He stoops and with his big gloves brushes away some snow, and a face comes out, a boy. The co-driver covers the small face again and says to Christa T.: That's what would have happened. She's alive; and perhaps he died while she was asleep. She insists on taking him with her, but mightn't the load get too heavy as time went by? Curious how he is there again ten years later, when she sees a rotting gas mask in a peaceful forest, on a road that brings her again into contact with the world's darker half from which she always wanted to escape . . .

More of that when the time comes. And to be told prudently, if possible, because the dead are easily wounded, it's obvious. What a live person can tell, being alive, would finally kill a dead person: flippancy. Therefore, one cannot, unfortunately, cling to the facts, which are too mixed up with chance and don't tell much. But it also becomes harder to keep things separate: what one knows with certainty, and since when; what she herself revealed, and what others revealed; what her writings add and what they hide; and what it is that one has to invent, for the truth's sake: the truth of that being who does now appear to me at times, and whom I approach with caution.

The paths we really took are overlaid with paths we did not take. I can now hear words that we never spoke. Now I can see her as she was, Christa T., when no witnesses were present. Could it be possible? —The years that re-ascend are no longer the years they were. Light and shadow fall once more over our field of vision: but the field is ready. Should that not amaze us?

3

We'd forgotten how to be in readiness even for miracles to happen.

We did hope for some support from chance. Could anyone, in his immense confusion, ever have taken heart and said "It had to be thus, and only thus"? Sometimes in a place one had long been familiar with, one could raise one's head, suddenly look about, and think: So this is where it has brought me . . .

On the blackboard in the large lecture hall stood a scanned line of verse: *Úns hât der winter geschâdet überál.* No writing on the wall, this, nothing in the least symbolic; and nothing in me was responding. I was listening to the lecturer, who wore a blue shirt, was red-haired and freckled, and showed great enthusiasm for the children's playground which he wanted the students of our faculty to build. No, I felt nothing, and I wasn't startled and I had no doubts. I saw Christa T. sitting in front of me. I could have put my hand on her shoulder, but didn't. It isn't her, I told myself, against my better knowledge, for it was her hand that I saw, writing. When she left, I stayed where I was. I didn't call her. I told myself: If it's her, then I'll see her every day. It was amazing, but I wasn't amazed; and the excitement I was waiting for never came.

If it was her—my God, it was her!—I wanted her to recognize me first. I knew that in seven years you can forget many names and faces, if you want to. In those days we economized strictly with our memories.

Then unexpectedly we were facing one another in the narrow aisle of a department store. Both at the same moment and spontaneously we signaled our recognition. It was her and it was me too. Yes, she too admitted that she'd recognized me at the lecture. The fact that we didn't ask one another why we had left it until now, in this place, to talk to one another, was the first sign of our old and now new intimacy.

We left the store and walked slowly through the streets of Leipzig, still a strange place for me, toward the station.

Resurrected from the dead. If miracles could happen, this was one of them; but we no longer knew the right way to accommodate a miracle. We hardly realized that a miracle can be met other than with broken phrases and mocking looks. We crossed the empty squares where the wind was still blowing, the wind that rises out of the ruins every day in cities after a war. Dust swept along the streets in front of us, gusts of wind blowing everywhere, it wasn't very comfortable; we turned up our coat collars and buried our hands in our pockets. And we used those broken phrases and temporizing looks which suit such cities best.

As Christa T. walked, she leaned slightly forward, as against some slight but permanent obstacle to which she'd grown accustomed. I supposed it was because of her height. Hadn't she always walked like this? She looked at me, smiled.

Now I knew too why I had prevented myself from talking to her straightaway. And this seemed the right moment to ask the question that occurred to me. But I didn't ask the question—either then or later; and only in my last letter, which she could no longer read, did I give a hint of it.

For the time being, the gap in our conversation had to be filled with information about ourselves: where she had ended up, and where I had. As if surprised, we shook our heads over the strange courses our lives had taken during the past six years, several times almost crossing. But almost isn't really, we knew that now, and fifty miles can be the same as five hundred. To have missed something by a lifetime is the same as missing it by a hair's breadth, we had found out about that; but we now acted as if we could still be surprised by the one mile which had prevented us from meeting earlier. Acted as if we really did want to know what had become of everything, though we didn't say much about things, and that gave us away. She now heard of our teacher's death, unless she knew of it before. Ah, Christa T. said. We gave one another a quick look. A distant death.

So there we were, asking one another about our experiences, as if conclusions could be drawn from them. Doing so, we noticed we were using and avoiding the same words. We'd both been to the same lecture; we must both have read the same books. There weren't many ways to choose among, at that time; no great choice among thoughts, hopes, doubts.

But one thing I really did want to know: was she still capable, at any moment, in the middle of the crowded street, among the hurrying, shabbily dressed people, of letting go with her shout—*hooohaahooo* . . . ? Or had I found her again in vain? Other people I had met in the meantime could do many of the other things. Only she could do that.

Had I missed feeling joy? Surprise? Suddenly the joy came. And even surprise arrived, late as usual. A miracle! If miracles could happen, this was one. And who says we weren't ready for it and met it inappropriately, with broken phrases? We stood at the streetcar stop and began to laugh. All the days ahead of us! We looked at one another and laughed, as at a successful prank, an utter trick, played on someone, perhaps on oneself. We were laughing as we said goodbye. She was laughing and waving to me as I left in the streetcar.

The laughter could stay. But we still had to travel once more the road from the store to the station, speak different words, finally find the courage to make whole sentences out of the broken ones, to eliminate the vagueness in our talk, however long it took. We have to look at one another differently, and see different things. Only the laughter at the end can stay the same: because all the days are ahead of us. All the time that will take away the vagueness, whether we like it or not. We'd better like it.

Better to travel the road twice, in that case.

Vagueness? The word may seem strange. The years we'd have had to talk about had been precise and sharp enough. But to make the precise and sharp cut-off separating "ourselves" from "the others," once and for all, that would save us. And secretly to know: the cut-off very nearly never came, because we ourselves might well have become otherwise. But how does one cut oneself away from oneself? We didn't speak of that. But she knew it, Christa T., when she walked beside me across the windy squares, or else we'd have had nothing to say. Her quick look, when we mentioned our teacher's death—a hard and distant death—proved one thing to me: she knew what it is, this innocence that comes from not being mature.

When we met and took that road a second time, Horst Binder, our railwayman neighbor's son, rose up again between us. Christa T. knew him too; I had pointed him out to her, had told her how he kept following me around. I was furious, a conquest like that doesn't do anything for one; he was creepy, he was nothing to boast about. He'd wanted to carry my book bag and I'd torn it out of his hand; I hated his wispy hair, which fell over his eyes, and most of all I hated his meaningful ardent look. I wanted to be able to laugh about him together with Christa T.; but she hadn't been able to laugh either, she'd been sorry for him.

Until one day we'd been out on parade, a huge square of white blouses and brown skirts. The one-armed troop commander bellowed a name so you could hear it all over the parade ground: Horst Binder. I knew what was coming. For he lived next door, and people on our street had been talking about him for days; but I couldn't speak his name any more, so I never mentioned him, not even to Christa T. I avoided her questioning look and wished what I shouldn't have wished: that I wasn't standing here in this troop, and that he, Horst Binder, wasn't about to be commended by the troop commander for denouncing his father, a railway workman, for listening to foreign radio stations.

I never did find out if she understood why we avoided looking one another in the eye when the time came to dismiss. Now, walking once more from the store to the station, I could tell her that in the end, before the Red Army arrived, Horst Binder had shot first his mother and then himself. We could ask one another why we'd been spared, why the opportunities had not swept us up as well. What opportunities would we have taken: all or none? And if we didn't know that, did we know anything about ourselves?

This terrible gratitude for the lack of opportunity isn't something to be forgotten. And this suspicion directed toward the adult in oneself . . . Proceed with all severity and sharpness against that adult: pour suspicion on him, accuse him, find him guilty. Don't tolerate any contradictions. Reject the defense with derision; pronounce the verdict: a life term. Accept it. Execute the verdict oneself.

Life term. Not an empty phrase.

Seven years later, walking a certain road, a broken phrase

is proof enough that this too is something we both understand.

As for Christa T., she'd had a breakdown during those years. It wasn't the work, although it may have been hard going, cutting out uniforms on the Mecklenburg farm, at a scratched wooden table, while summer came on, in spite of everything. Sometimes the young Soviet lieutenant came, stood in the doorway, looked in her direction, looked at her; neither knew what the other was thinking. Once he shook her hand, before he left: Why are you so sad? Then she ran home, threw herself on the bed, bit the pillows; then nothing was any use, she screamed. Good heavens, so sensitive too! And always for no reason.

The horseman who'd done nothing but gallop across a lake that happened to be frozen over fell dead from his horse when he discovered what he'd crossed. She only screamed, it's not much. She burned her old diaries, all her vows went up in smoke, and the enthusiasms one was now ashamed of, the aphorisms and songs. There won't be time for her to speak of them again, *her* lifetime's not long enough. On that subject, meanwhile, only broken phrases.

Then came one summer when we were less than thirty miles apart, working in fields that were quite similar to one another. She must have noticed that one can breathe here too, that the lungs are also made for this new air. To live thus, straighten one's back, dripping sweat, look about oneself. This kind of country. Fields, meadow, a few bushes, the river. Lean cows with black spots, fenced enclosures. This foreign flickering heat, which leaps about between sky and earth far away on the horizon, unmitigated, uncooled by the forest which, in her deepest convictions, ought to limit the view on all sides. Vanquish the feeling that it's indecent for the land to turn to the sky, nakedly, baldly, directly, without the mediation of trees. Look up. But not into the sun, it'll kill me. It'll liquefy the blue, make it metallic and watery, it doesn't want us to have the blue, I can't bear it, this longing for the real blue, but I'll go fetch it, now, just a second . . . Yes.

They put her in a truck and drove off. You see, she's not up to it. Looks strong, but she's delicate inside, or something. She should do what the burgomaster suggested. Can't make much difference to her, to take a teacher re-training course. Can't she see what's with the children hereabouts? All right then, she says, I'll teach, why not. —She gave me a sideways look to see if I understood that she felt uneasy about grabbing the first thing to come along, especially this thing, which, as she knew, can't be done by halves. A teacher! I said. What a stroke of luck!

I have a picture of her taken at that time.

Yes, perhaps what she was looking for among the children was shelter. Their light precarious breath, their small hands holding one's own. And the fact that only important things are important to them. Love, for example, she can't help still believing in it, somewhat. When doubts came— love, what is it? can it help to shift a single speck of dust?— then sometimes she thought back on the little schoolhouse, the thirty-two children facing her, on decrepit old benches, poorly dressed, hungry, and, oh God, their shoes! But to offer them shelter with one's own unshelteredness . . .

Three years. Her attic room with the sloping walls, the piles of shoddily bound books with thick gray pages, the new names on the covers, Gorky, Makarenko, the new pamphlets which everyone was given, as important as one's daily bread, unless one's hand was shut. Curiously enough, she finds some of what she reads familiar; it dawns on her that such thoughts are possible; she doesn't understand how, after all this rational clarity, the uttermost unreason could still have been possible. She jumps up: yes, that's how it will be, this is the way to ourselves. Understood this way, her longing wouldn't be ridiculous and beside the point; it would be usable and helpful.

Not a word about this on our first walk. At most, two or

three titles, sober concepts from philosophy and economics. Would I understand? Know the pain of self-expansion, also the pleasure, which is unforgettable and by which one will measure all future pleasures? How many of them will have to be rejected. But she, Christa T., on our way to the station, pushes her coat collar up, before I can get too close to her. It's understood. Now what next?

But in that earlier time, looking up from the precise and illuminating statements in the pamphlets, she walks to the window of her room. The view overlooking seventeen poplar trees. The tallest is being climbed today by the shepherd's son, a boy in my class, and he drags down the magpie's nest, to shouts of encouragement from a gang of boys at the foot of the tree. But he flings the eggs, almost ready for hatching, one after another against the big boulder which served at last week's lesson on the geology of the region. And there I stand, have read my pamphlets, look on while it's happening, and it makes me want to cry. It's such a thin surface we walk on, so close to our feet the danger of dropping through into this bogland. Hurl the tomcat against the stable wall, leave the boy lying there in the snow, throw the bird's eggs against the boulder. Every time it happens she's cut to the quick.

Her picture. The face of the teacher, Christa T., "Miss T.," twenty-one years old, among thirty-two children's faces, with the brick wall of the schoolhouse behind. At this very moment they too may be standing there to be photographed, the children of the ten-year-olds of that time, and their teacher will be twenty-one years old, but she looks different. I'd like to walk through the village and ask the people who are now around thirty: Do you remember her, know her? At least her name? Have you remembered, at least, perhaps, that she implored you not to drown the kittens in the river, not to chase the blind old dogs and throw stones at them, not to throw the young birds against the wall? Did you laugh at her? Or you girls, whose women's faces are shimmering through on this picture, didn't you find yourselves thinking of her when you held your own children in your arms?

The children's faces. Some laughing, some self-satisfied, some frightened, one with a threatening look, a few sinister, but I can't find anything that's mysterious. The teacher, top row, extreme left, is different. She has something to hide, a wound, one might think, slow to heal. She's aloof and restrained, but ready. Being depended upon, she found a foothold. Being asked a favor, she smiles. The eyes, of course . . .

Is that the place for her to stay in? Three successive years she joins her class, before the summer holidays, the photographer snaps the shutter, develops the plate, he sees no difference, delivers the pictures and takes his fee. The teacher, Christa T., goes into her room and ranges the three photos beside one another, looks at them for a long time, you couldn't notice a tremor. Finally she sits down at her desk, the pictures in front of her, and writes her application for admission to the university.

That's how she came to be in the same lecture hall as I, to face the same blackboard, the same freckled boy who insists on building a children's playground with us. His name is Günter, Christa T. says—we've almost reached the station—I know him, there's no stopping him. That's the moment we start to laugh, and we go on laughing, until my streetcar comes.

All the days ahead of us!

4

Christa T. was timid.

Mainly it was the fear that one might vanish without trace, a frequent enough event in those days. She compulsively left traces, hasty and careless ones, so that the right hand needn't know what the left hand is doing; so that at any moment one can blot everything out again, preferably even hiding the traces from oneself; so that nobody is obliged, either, to find one, unless he's making a special search—but who'd follow such faint traces as those left by unadmitted fear . . . Who could have anticipated that she'd cover so much paper with her writings? Krischan, why don't you write? Yes, yes, she said, didn't argue, didn't agree. Waited. For a long time had no notion what she might be waiting for, I'm certain. She must have realized early in her life that we aren't capable of saying things exactly as they are. Maybe one can even realize this too soon and be discouraged forever after; maybe one can become clear-sighted too early in life, too soon bereft of self-delusion. So that one gives up and lets things take their course. Then things have no way out: they can be neither imprecise nor false . . . Then they make the best they can of themselves, or the worst. Or mediocrity results, which is often the worst thing. Yet mediocrity, if that's the threat one feels, isn't something to be passed over in silence.

To think that I can only cope with things by writing! Was that really a reproach? Does this secret self-reproach explain the state of the writings she left? Of the diaries, sketches, observations, stories, lists of titles, the drafts and letters? Such carelessness, it can't be camouflaged as disorder or haste. It shimmers through, that weakness she reproached: writing—her supposed self-defense against the superior power of things. And despite it all, she did cope. She didn't know she could say that of herself.

It occurs to me that we could never ask her: What are you going to be? One can ask this of others without fear of touching on something impossible to express. We sat facing one another upstairs in our local café (Christa T. had changed universities, also her field of study, she was between the third and fourth year when I met her again); she was leafing through her notebooks. She's often to be seen sitting at this round, marble-topped table in the corner, with various other people, who are her friends, not one another's. Also she sits there alone, she seems to be busy. She's "preparing"—for what? With the last penny of her scholarship money she pays for the cheap dark cake she eats; she's doing what everyone else does, why shouldn't one ask her, as long as it's with a laugh: What are you going to be, Krischan? She lowers her notebook with a movement one wishes one hadn't seen, and she's forgotten all about the seminar that was bothering her, she looks for a long time out of the window, at people walking singly or in groups out of the dark lane opposite, people saying goodbye, waving to one another, or walking along together: it couldn't be a more ordinary sight. But what was she seeing?

Well? —Her familiar look, dark, a little scornful, somewhat reproachful. Me? Teacher, maybe? she might ask. One gave up, said nothing more, let the matter rest, didn't insist on anything definite, because it was perfectly plain—she really couldn't know. She did try to fit in; what made her different wasn't mere disdain. She had the best intentions of providing herself with one of the classifications which suited other people so excellently; she marked it down as a deficiency in herself, not to be able to give a straight answer—teacher, management trainee, university lecturer, publisher's reader . . .

She didn't trust these names, oh no. She didn't trust herself. She was doubtful, amid our toxic swirl of new name-giving; what she doubted was the reality of names, though she had to deal with them; she certainly felt that naming is seldom accurate and that, even if it is accurate, name and thing coincide only for a short time. She shrank from stamping any name on herself, the brand mark which decides which herd you belong to and which stable you should occupy. *Life, to live it through, free vast life! O glorious sense of living, don't ever leave me. Simply to be a human being* . . .

What are you going to be, Krischan? A human being? Well, you know . . .

She had to be going. She admitted that she really must go and study. She disappeared for days. She was studying, so she said, and we pretended to believe her. Then she showed up again, just before the exams. We'd gone over all our work already, exchanged notebooks, made extracts and card indexes, formed study groups and vowed that nobody would get less than a B+ average. Then she reappeared and asked, all innocence, for the topics. We hid our despair. Instead of asking her at the next group meeting where on earth she had been, what she'd been doing all this time, instead of making her recognize her responsibility, everyone gave her his notes, offered to help. Günter, our freckled secretary, gave her his outlines: showed her how a bad mark from her would lower the seminar's average. Did she really want that? —Heavens no, said Christa T., you're all so efficient! She went to see a friend, Gertrud Born, and had herself tested on the metrics of the Merseburg *Zaubersprüche;* obediently she declaimed *"Ik gihôrta d'at seggen,"* and it was getting late, she had to be chaperoned back to her lodging. It turned out that she'd been reading Dostoevsky and was now giving much thought to the proposition that extreme softness vanquishes extreme hardness. It was a very important question: was the proposition true in all circumstances?

They had reached her door. Then she walked Gertrud home again and was thinking aloud, on the way, about how one could make a whole life out of the bits one was presented with, and whether such wholeness was really the aim . . . If not, then what is? Then back they walked to her house together. The city was silent now. Far off, a streetcar rattled down the main street. Tired, she leaned against a wall covered with posters. Lights were still burning in a few windows. Why were people still up? Was her restlessness spreading, infecting everyone? And how can one give people the courage to be restless? *Longing, blackbird in the night, you have the lightest sleep . . .*

She hardly ever talked about love. She kept herself to herself; nothing remarkable about that. She was looking after our child once and she seemed so absorbed that I asked her outright. That's hard to explain, she said. Although, this time, you know, I'm almost certain. I think, she added as an afterthought.

And you know what you're talking about?

She smiled. But neither of us thought of the time we'd leaned against the school wall; her superiority was gone now, and it was I who had to put the question. Anyway,

36

when I compared my life with hers, I thought I was entitled now to ask if she knew what she was talking about.

Maybe, she said. And that there'd been one or two occasions.

I named a name.

Not him, she said. A while ago, one summer. Love in the summertime, and so on. But then she added: It's a difficult story. It was such a long time ago. —She picked up her book and lapsed into silence.

A difficult story. But not tellable at all under the disheartening pressure of facts we are fortunately ignorant of. It might have been her last summer in the village. An evening toward the end of June. She was standing, if we so choose, by the fence among the cherry trees in the school garden—which, as we do know, are authentic; likewise the duck pond on which her back is turned. The frogs haven't begun to croak yet. He was cycling down the road, she saw him when he was still some way off; perhaps she was thinking: So he did decide to come, today of all days. Or she didn't think it, she just sensed it. As he put on the brakes and jumped off, she handed him a few cherries over the fence. Here's your wages for coming, she said, and saw herself standing by the fence and handing cherries to a man, couldn't help laughing, for you can't come to any harm as long as you can still see yourself standing there.

But he didn't notice the cherries, he wanted to know if it was true. —It'll be true all right, she said, if it makes you as angry as that. What are you talking about?

You're leaving us, he said.

If that's how you want to put it, said Christa T., then true is what it is.

Why? he must have asked. Have we done anything to offend you?

Then she must have laughed. And when he insists on asking why, all she can reply with is another question: Are you really interested in knowing? She knows this is the way to do it, and she wants, just for once, to have done it; wants to keep her gaze resting on his, and walk the few paces along the fence to the gate, unlatch the gate, in thought, and now stand beside him on the path that leads around the village, sensing that she's a little over half a head shorter than he is, good proportions. And you can't come to any harm as long as you're still busy measuring.

And you? Christa T. says, to keep the conversation going at least. You're not leaving? What about the holidays?

Me? Leave here? No.

She sighs. Here's a man who knows what he wants. Between two houses they turn off and take the cross-country path. Gorse bushes to left and right, faded already. Jasmine hedgerows, over which, a little laboriously, threatened or enticed by subsidence, the sun is still standing. That would be a nice oil painting, says Christa T. thoughtfully, but she doesn't let him notice that she enjoys making fun; after all, he's so deeply serious. —So he's become accustomed to living here?

Completely, he answers. Forever, I think. What are you laughing about? I've got my reasons.

I don't doubt it.

Now you're making fun of me.

That, my dear man, was the first serious remark I've made, but you didn't notice it. She heard how he said "forever" and it had given her a pang, just for a moment. Nothing can come of it, there's nothing between us, it can't be, mustn't be.

You know why, he said. The school. It can be developed, that's for sure. But it's all up to me, including the school garden, believe it or not.

I can believe it, says Christa T. She takes another look at him. The new young school principal from the next village.

Blue suits you, she says. —That's how it's done, that's right, says the voice inside her, but now she silences it.

Blue! he shouts, in despair. My old shirt! If I'd known, I'd have put a completely different . . .

Completely is your favorite word, isn't it? Christa T. asks.

You're the only person who asks questions like that, he says, quietly and bitterly. I've noticed it: you don't like things to be completely right or completely in order.

You're wrong there, she says gravely. I'd have liked it a lot if I'd ever found it anywhere. But what made you notice it?

Ah, he murmurs. Often. When the school inspector gives us a talk, for instance. You don't ever laugh, no, it's not that. But I can see it: you have your doubts.

Not always, she says. If you'd been watching more closely you'd realize that I make my comparisons. I compare my school with what the inspector says.

Just look here a moment, he bursts out. And I compare his talk with my dream of my school.

Funny, she says. That's something about you I like. She listens for the voice inside: nothing? Nothing.

Now the sun has sunk into the hedgerows. Best thing would be for them to run across the fields and for the spread hay to give off its fragrance. So off they run, and there's the fragrance of hay, everything's just as it should be. Now she must ask him about the poplar trees: Has he ever climbed poplar trees? —Oh yes, back home . . .

I didn't put it the right way. Have you never robbed a magpie's nest? Have you never thrown the young birds against the stable wall?

To be quite honest, he says awkwardly, I could never do it. I'm funny about things like that, you know.

And people?

What do you mean, he'll probably ask, and he'll know what she means. Three years after the war, people know what you mean when you ask a question like that.

You were in the army, she'll have explained.

I was lucky, he says. After a moment he added: Sometimes I've thought that a girl would ask me that one day.

They're sitting on the edge of the meadow now, and

Christa T., who has forgotten how one does it, begins to wonder: so that's all there is to it, all foreseen, step by step and piece by piece, and I confess it's soothing when nothing unforeseeable happens the first time.

Now it has happened, she reminds him: a girl has asked you.

That's true, he says almost sadly. And I was hardly aware.

Hardly aware of what? The girl or the question?

Both, he answered.

But she's thinking: that's how it goes—all unawares, but all foreseen. I couldn't wish for anything better.

Show me your hands, she says.

He simply does so. Either you've had a very bad time, he says, or else it was nothing.

Very bad, she says. It was nothing.

You're very curious, he says. And I know that you'll leave, whatever happens. I can't keep you.

No, you can't keep me.

Now he asks: Must I pass three test questions?

Good, three questions.

Now the sun is only a hand's breadth above the horizon. Any amount of time.

The first: What was I just thinking?

You think day and night that you'll leave here, come what may, and nobody can stop you.

The second: What will become of me?

You want me to tell you that, he says bitterly. And that question was wrongly put. You should have asked: What must become of me? Otherwise I'd have known.

Third, says Christa T., what does a human being need?

A task, he says, sure that he's right this time.

It's your own fault, she says. Such tests never end unambiguously, and you knew it. The sun has gone down, and nothing has been decided. Make a note of that.

I knew it, says the man beside her. She hears him standing up.

Stay, she says. Stay.

It had to be she who did the choosing, here and always.

Of course, she said, I can't promise anything.

It was like that, or maybe it was different. In that year or the next. That man or another. Love in the summertime, she later says to me. The summer will have been not long and not short, the love not too difficult and not too easy, the next village, or whatever it was, not too near and not too far. The path around the village familiar, yet strange. And she knowing herself much too well, and painfully ignorant of herself.

That's what she had of it; it's how I want it. She must have learned what she had to know; and then she must have left. A difficult story.

She came to the city and was alone for a long time.

To my surprise I see that both these facts need some explanation, though at that time both seemed equally revealing. Her sister, who was one year older, whom she dearly loved, may have asked her pressing questions or even warned her, knowing what they shared, worrying that she might overdo things, as could easily happen. Her father, hardly explicit, but alluding to his frailty, suggested that she might be a welcome successor to him at his school. Her mother, who was more explicit, when they were alone together might have asked: Would she be left all alone? And what would become of the house they lived in as part of the schoolteacher's contract?

Even then Christa left. Later she often repeated this procedure—of going away—and there's a pattern to be read here, even on first sight: you leave what you know too well, leave what has ceased to be a challenge. Keep alive your curiosity about other ranges of experience, and ultimately about yourself in any new circumstances. Prefer the movement to the goal. —Such a nature has obvious drawbacks for its surroundings and itself.

In those days this hardly attracted much attention. Everyone was under pressure to move on and had to keep up the courage to do so; time passed very quickly. One didn't spend much time reflecting, one virtually fished out a life for oneself, without looking, hardly ever asked if it suited oneself, simply lived it, and so it came to suit one. That was what one thought as time went by, anyway.

Of course external circumstances militated against this, ridiculously so. Christa T., in the rebuilt city, looked at rooms, landladies. She realized that she mustn't expect seventeen poplar trees; she'd prefer not to look out of the window at all. She pushed out her lower lip, all right, and she took the room. The street was named after a German philosopher. On some evenings a child would come and carefully wash the ornamental stonework in the treeless and shrubless front yard. In the early morning, armies of housewives would beat their carpets in every yard of the neighborhood. And her landlady would appear in the door, a letter between pointed fingertips, or with a motto for the wall under her arm: Christa T. had just taken the motto down and placed it outside in the corridor. "Even if Hope's last Anchor breaks, Courage, Courage is What it Takes." How can it be? Don't you like this one either? Do you mean to tell me you can live without any spiritual comfort? Frau Schmidt, split in half, one half landlady and the other exposed to the temptation of human kindness, thus subject to being played off against herself. When she leaves Christa T.'s room she doesn't recognize herself. With her own bare hands she carries the motto away again; and she wonders what she has just consented to. Quickly she fetches a hammer and knocks a nail into the wall where there's an empty space in the long corridor: there the motto will hang, conspicuous among the other notices saying when the lodgers have to be home by (alone, of course); when, please, the light must be switched off; how often the toilet can be used; and how much water can be used for what purposes.

Bürger, schützt eure Anlagen! says Christa T., and laughs in tidy property-protecting Frau Citizen Schmidt's face. To no purpose, naturally. For in the long run nobody can live in the world as it is without knowing exactly what's forbidden and what is not. So I'm doing my lodgers a good turn and relieving them of doubts.

Christa T. lived for three years in Frau Schmidt's house.

5

We don't know much about those years; for one has no real
knowledge of things as yet unstated; nor do we know if
stating a thing makes it a certainty. My own hesitation tells
me that the time hasn't yet come to tell with ease and flu-
ency about everything one could or did observe at first hand.
So why tell of anything at all? With such a handicap,
wouldn't it be better to remain silent?

Yes: if one had any choice. But it is Christa T. herself
who keeps implicating me. The fact that she really lived and
really died almost without being recognized is anything but
an invention. Now, if I look up for a moment, I can see her
walking in front of me: she never turns around, but I have
to follow her, down and back, even when I begin to realize
where it's all leading and what she intended of me, from the
start. As if she, of all the exemplary people (and that's what
writing means—to furnish examples), she was the one who

suggested herself. She, Christa T., to whom we can't apply a single one of the laudatory words which our time and we ourselves have quite justifiably produced. Although one or two of them might suit her a little, perhaps more than a little, albeit their usual sense would have to be changed. Ah, if I could freely and happily choose to invent without being ambiguous . . .

It would never have occurred to me, I swear, to think of her as an exemplary person. For she isn't an exemplary case at all. I won't say that the same could be presumed of every real and living person; and I profess the freedom and responsibility of invention. Just for once, for this once, I want to discover how it is and to tell it like it is: the unexemplary life, a life that can't be used as a model.

Christa T., as she then was, must have been wrong about herself for years; and she paid for this, as a person with a strong sense of reality does pay for illusions of all sorts, and pays most dearly for illusions about himself. I didn't notice anything: I found it natural for her to want to be like everyone else. I might ask why I didn't notice anything, or precious little. Hadn't we rediscovered one another? Hadn't we finally found, when we met again, the right words, or at least the right laughter? Surprise, joy? And intimacy? Yes, we had, to a certain extent. Since I'm alive and she isn't, I can decide what's to be talked about and what is not. That is the disregard the living show for the dead. And it is our right, the right of not wanting to know, of not having to say. A reasonable right.

Perhaps, things being as they are, I shouldn't assume all the responsibility. I could visit witnesses who are still alive, as is proper for friends of a person who died young. Could go to the city where we were students together. Walk across the square by the university. Unless I'm utterly mistaken, there'd be flower beds there now, not the clumsy homemade arrangements of our godchildren's playground, in which Günter, Günter with the freckles, devoutly planted tomatoes and scarlet runners. It's certain to make me laugh. I shall

45

notice that the dust which used to blow across the square and always made us cross it in a hurry has now been well and truly laid. That was the last thing I'd have expected; but the flower beds explain that too.

The interior of the building I would find, moreover, not much changed, less changed than one might wish. The inside courtyard still not used, not even by the new generation, and still marked off-limits by the sign reading *Caution Danger of Falling Masonry*—although it's hardly probable that the war-damaged roof will cave in after more than twenty years in its present state. Today's students would, like ourselves in our time, pass it by unawares, and they'd pass me by too; I'd have to give myself a shake and realize they can't see me as their contemporary, though that is what I have become these past weeks, in a disturbing sort of way. On the staircase—the same worn-down stone steps, the same draft blowing through the unrepaired roof—I'd ask one of the students to direct me to Dr. Dölling's office. His answer would come without hesitation, unlike my question, for I first have to brush aside the image of the slender pale Gertrud Born before I can speak her new name and new title without faltering. Naturally I'd find her in the room where one found the lecturers ten or eleven years ago. I'd knock and walk in, Gertrud Born would look up and recognize me. It would make a great difference if I could tell whether her joy was real or feigned.

Let's suppose her joy is real. After a few moments she'd be wondering why Christa T. particularly, among all our other acquaintances, interested me. Dr. Dölling would be discreet and not intrusive; that was my own rule too. Although—why else should I go to her? She, Gertrud Born, would certainly know how one has to look to be worthy of the work of "construction," as she would probably say. If she could stand up, emerge from behind her desk, leave her fortress—the few paces across the room to the group of armchairs by the window could be enough to bring her back into the construction. The woman walking over there is Dr.

Dölling, a well-groomed woman, not a person with a plenitude of being to draw on but a person who doesn't hide the talent she's endowed with. She alone knows what it has cost her to be rid of the pale, nondescript Gertrud Born, to suppress her shyness, to learn how to walk as she now can; and she doesn't want anyone else to know. While sitting across from her, I'd have to respect that.

Christa T., hm. Gertrud Dölling will be defensive, and I shan't know why, but I shall curse myself for having come here at all.

She was, she'll say, different from the others. But you know that. She never liked coordination. She never worked regularly—she couldn't.

And you, Gertrud, with all your discipline, you bore the burden and nobody ever heard you complain.

She was a curious person, Gertrud Dölling would say. And I'd have to give her a long questioning look before she came out with the next words: I might say she was—unbalanced.

I let the word evaporate; it doesn't belong in this room and has soon disappeared.

I might say: That was what you were always saying. When I remind Gertrud Dölling of this, she laughs and places her fingertips together, just as Gertrud Born always did when she was embarrassed.

What was it threatened the balance?

Dr. Dölling usually thinks quickly and precisely and formulates the results. Now she might hesitate.

Her imagination, she'll perhaps say, not quite content with herself. She was—eccentric. She never managed to recognize the limits which, after all, everyone does have. She lost herself in everything, you only had to wait for it. Sometimes you had the impression that all the studying, all the book stuff, didn't really concern her at all. She was after something else. And that—I almost took it as an offense, you know.

She gave me a quick look. That'll be the moment at

which I look down, or so I suppose, for it's unthinkable that I could sit there calmly and hear her announce my own feelings.

Gertrud Born always blushed easily; now she stands up and walks to the window. But I finally see the role Christa T. played in her life: she made it questionable for her. And pale, shy Gertrud Born stood it for three years; she actually wanted it so, if my thinking is correct. At this point I shall begin to respect her. But of course I shall have to calm her, at the expense of truth.

Well, I shall say, she simply had too many interests; she never had the wisdom of self-restraint; and often enough that was the reproach she leveled against herself.

Mad, I shall think, we're starting already to hide her away, to sacrifice the dead for the living who can't use the whole truth. —But once more I'd been wrong about Gertrud Born.

Oh no, she'll say, with a peculiar simplicity. She had only one interest: people. Perhaps she was studying the wrong subject—literature. What can it have meant to her? But what would the right subject have been?

Should one, against all expectation, now have to wonder about this together with Gertrud Dölling?

As a matter of fact, she'll probably say now, she had nobody but me in those days.

No, I won't contradict her, but I won't let it go at that. Kostia, I'll say. Don't forget Kostia.

Then, naturally, she'll shake her head. Her old perseverance has become obstinacy.

No, she'll say, there wasn't anyone besides me. Kostia! Can you really take that whirligig of a relationship seriously?

I shall lapse into silence, for I have Christa T.'s diaries.

So then she really didn't have anybody, and my attempt to justify her—why else should I have visited Gertrud Dölling?—has come to nothing. Why should I go on listening?

You think as she used to, Gertrud Dölling will say: that everything depends on how you look at it; her relationship with Kostia, for instance. But that isn't the point, it never is. That was a trait of hers, too: to disregard the objective facts. Then came the miserable after-effects, talking and talking . . .

Hangover? I shall ask cautiously.

More than once. This ocean of sadness! Simply because people didn't want to be as she saw them.

Or, I shall suggest, because she couldn't be as we wanted her to be?

Gertrud Dölling understands, but she's beyond this kind of argument. As we wanted? she'll vehemently reply. Wanted? Did we ever have any choice? Weren't we forced to do the first things first, as well as we could, and to ask for nothing more, over and over? Haven't the results been astounding achievements? Or could things be better than they are today?

But that wasn't my question. Where's this getting us, I shall think, and I shall ask Gertrud Dölling, considerately: What are you reproaching her for?

Reproaching whom, she'll say, and she's confused. Oh, I see. Her. You must have misunderstood me. Reproach. Don't forget, we were friends, real friends. She could always depend on me.

And that's true. When Christa T. became restless, when she began to skitter about, when she disappeared and then came back later, strange, as if she'd been away for a long time—she could always be sure that Gertrud Born had stayed put and was waiting for her, immutable in loyalty and love, that no questions would be asked and no explanations expected, she was understood without having to explain.

What's left for me to do but stand up and quietly leave?

What do I reproach her for? says Gertrud Dölling from the window she's standing next to, and her voice has changed. For dying, for really dying. She always did everything as if it was for fun, as an experiment. She could always stop one thing and then start something quite different. Not many people can do that. And then she lies down and dies in all seriousness and she can't stop doing that. —Or do you think that she died of this sickness?

No.

I shan't go to her, shan't visit Gertrud Dölling. The conversation won't take place, we'll save ourselves the emotions. And the question, what Christa T. died of, I shall ask on my own account, in due course, without doubting that the sickness, leukemia, was the thing she couldn't deal with or bring to a stop.

I shall stay home. Why should I make Gertrud Dölling sad? She's everything she can be. Not many people can say of themselves, as she can, that they attain their limits. And certain questions I wanted to ask her I can just as well, or better, ask myself. The detour was superfluous.

Moreover, all questions lose their edge in time; and language allows the evasive use of "we" in place of "I," nearly always, never with so much justification as when talking of that time. So that a person must never be asked to take over someone else's liabilities, except perhaps in some circumstances.

Of course I believed that Christa T. and I were still friends. She didn't attach any special hopes, I now know, to my reappearance. Only later did she begin to take me into account, even then only for certain stretches of time; in between, she could set herself adrift again. I've discovered letters in which I warn her: for the last time, again and again for the last time. Then comes a feeble letter of apology from her: If only I could pull myself together . . .

The truth is: we had other things to do. We were fully occupied with making ourselves unassailable—perhaps the sense of that can be felt. Not only to admit into our minds nothing extraneous—and all sorts of things we considered extraneous; also to let nothing extraneous well up from inside ourselves, and if it did so—a doubt, a suspicion, observations, questions—then not to let it show. Less from fear, although many people were frightened, than from insecurity. A feeling of insecurity that is more difficult to shed than anything else I know.

Except certainty, which is the other side of the coin. How can that possibly be explained. It's simply so.

For the new world that we were making and making unassailable—even if it meant building ourselves into the foundations of it—that world really did exist. It exists, and not only in our heads; and that period was for us the beginning of it. But whatever happened or will happen to that new world is and remains our affair. Among the alternatives offered there isn't a single one that's worth a nod in its direction . . .

What she wished for more intensely than anything, and I'm speaking now of Christa T., was the coming of our world; and she had precisely the kind of imagination one needs for a real understanding of it. Whatever they may say, the new world of people without imagination gives me the shudders. Factual people. Up-and-doing people, as she called them. And in her dark moments she felt inferior to them. Also she did try to accommodate herself to them, to acquire a profession that would have brought her into public life: with this aim she surprised and outsmarted even herself. And she compelled herself to be rational. She set limits to her propensity for gazing, dreaming, drifting. She did remove the painful barrier between thinking and doing. And she cut all compromises. *We must do something to make life worth living for all people. One must be ready to accept a certain degree of responsibility. Of course*—she immediately added—*one must have an unbroken view across that responsibility, and fulfill it completely, and not be lax about it* . . .

She joined in our discussions, those glorious rambling nocturnal discussions about the paradise on whose doorstep we were sure we stood, hungry. and wearing our wooden shoes. The idea of perfection had taken hold of our minds, had passed into us from our books and pamphlets; and from the rostrums at meetings came in addition a great impatience: verily, I say unto you, you shall be with me today in paradise! Oh, we had a presentiment of it, it was irrefutable and irreplaceable, we were making sure of it, by arguing whether or not our paradise would have atom-powered heating, or would it be gas? And would it pass through two stages of development, or more, and by what signs, when it finally arrived, would we be able to recognize it? Who, but who, would be worthy to inhabit it? Only the very purest, that seemed a certainty. So we subjected ourselves afresh to our exercises; today we smile when we remind one another about it. We become again, for a few moments, akin to one another, as we were for years by virtue of this faith of ours. Even today we can recognize one another by a phrase we use, or a slogan. Wink at one another. Paradise can make itself scarce, that's the way of it. Make a wry face if you like, but all the same: one must, once in a lifetime, when the time was right, have believed in the impossible.

6

What does the world need to become perfect?

This and this alone was the question which wrapped her
up in herself; but more deeply still it was the presumptuous
hope that she, Christa T. herself, might be necessary for the
world's perfection. Nothing less than this could validate her
life; the presumption is, of course, a daring one, and the
great danger was that she might overtax herself. They
weren't empty, the warnings that came from her sister, who
has stayed loyal to her village school and is even on the
verge of a sensible marriage. Christa T., in the letters she
writes to her, vacillates between envious admiration—how
efficient she is, her sister, she gets a hold on life, doesn't
abandon herself to fruitless ponderings—and the reproach
that her sister is satisfied too easily and too soon, is resigning
herself, not getting out of herself all that she might. But

what am I doing!—she writes at the end of one such letter. Not all the letters are sent, either.

She went to the lectures, sat in her seat in the reading room, followed with her eyes the ranks of book backs and was suddenly afraid that the books might contain answers to all the questions. She jumped up, ran out, traveled by streetcar all the way back into the city, it was foggy again, she was freezing cold.

Yesterday, she writes to her sister, *I walked home in the evening through the old part of the city. Was suddenly madly relaxed, landed in a damp sort of joint, the ladies and gentlemen stared at me. A traveling farmer from the Magdeburg region left his professional lady friend and came over to me. Eager for a jolly evening in Auerbach's Keller. We talked politics, which we found not so jolly, drank and smoked heavily at his expense, eventually I left him in the lurch and flitted away. —I smoke too much, am often dead beat and sad . . .*

A first symptom, isolated, unnoticed, which she couldn't explain. When you reach Trümoh, she told herself, kick off your slippers! Then she was on top of the world again, because, laughable as it may seem, she'd met her Indian: Klingsor—he couldn't have had any other name—with his fiery look, snow-white turban, and, unfortunately, holes in his socks, which she wasn't allowed to touch. Nobody will look after him, she told herself, and at the Book Fair she stayed close to him, for as long as she could without attracting attention. And even if she did, what did it matter? For of course he noticed her, and stopped, to see how far she'd follow him. And you won't believe it, she said, but he gave me a nod when we finally went our separate ways.

That night I dreamed about him. I dreamed that I met him again at the Technical Fair, where I've never been, and that he took my hand and led me to the engine-tool section: Come, my child, a poet must concern herself with neighboring disciplines . . . The next day, naturally, I went to the Technical Fair. And there he was, among the engine-tools.

He was no more surprised than I was, and he bowed to me like a real Klingsor.

No, I wasn't surprised. Feeling and dream hadn't deceived me.

She hadn't noticed or admitted what the whole dream was about. For only in this romantic disguise, among so many detailed safeguards, was the word allowed to emerge: someone had called her a poet, and she airily overlooked it. But she heard what she heard.

There's no sense now in being dismayed at her playing hide-and-seek with us all: she was playing it with herself too. How clearly I can see through all her evasions! Her attempts at withdrawal, I'd thwart them all now, if I could. But she has finally withdrawn. It was her sickness doing it, her sickness, Gertrud.

Remarkable or not—it was in those days that she began to write. Why remarkable? Shouldn't any time be an equally good or bad time for the attempt to search for yourself, inside and outside? For, as far as I can see, that was the case with her. Hard to understand today why there should be anything surprising about it.

Christa T. lived strenuously even when she seemed lackadaisical; that ought to be attested, though the point here cannot be to justify her: this isn't a trial, no verdict is given, on her or on anyone else, least of all on what we call "our time"—not a very meaningful phrase. She didn't attempt to escape from it all, as many people were starting to do in those years. When her name was called: "Christa T.!"—she stood up and went and did what was expected of her; was there anyone to whom she could say that hearing her name called gave her much to think about: Is it really me who's meant? Or is it only my name that's being used? Counted in with other names, industriously added up in front of the equals sign? And might I just as well have been absent, would anyone have noticed? She saw, too, how people began to slip away, leaving only the shell of a name behind. She couldn't do that.

But she also lost the capacity to live in a state of rapture. The vehement overplayed words, the waving banners, the deafening songs, the hands clapping rhythms over our heads. She felt how words begin to change when they aren't being tossed out any more by belief and ineptitude and excessive zeal but by calculation, craftiness, the urge to adapt and conform. Our words, not even false ones—how easy it would be if they were!—but the person speaking them has become a different person. Does that change everything?

Christa T. began, very early on, when one thinks about it today, to ask herself what change means. The new words? The new house? Machines, bigger fields? The new man, she heard people say; and she began to look inside herself.

For it wasn't easy to see people behind the gigantic cardboard placards they carried around, to which, remarkably, we got accustomed in the end. And about which we began to quarrel: who'd call them back to mind today if they'd really stayed outside and hadn't infiltrated among us by many and devious roads? So that it wasn't they who mistrusted us, not they and the frightful beaming heroes of newspapers, films, and books, but ourselves: we mistrusted ourselves, we had adopted their standard and began—in distress and terror—to compare ourselves with them. Inevitably the comparison was to our disadvantage. So there emerged around us, or in us too, it is the same thing, a hermetic space which had its own internal laws, with its stars and suns, revolving with apparent effortlessness around a center which was subject to no laws, to no change, and least of all to doubt. The machinery which made it all move—or did it move?—the cogs, chains, and rods, were submerged in darkness; one rejoiced in the absolute perfection and purposiveness of the apparatus, and to keep it going smoothly seemed worth any sacrifice, even the sacrifice achieved by self-extinction. And only today do we feel any proper surprise: feelings have to travel a long way.

What an idea: Christa T. pitting her "Child in the Evening" against this machinery. One shouldn't juxtapose effect and counter-effect so directly, no doubt; moreover, to be sure, she never put dates under what she'd written. But everything, the handwriting, the make and age of the paper, indicates that the sketches relating to her childhood were written at that time. Difficult to say if she took this juxtaposition seriously, or hid the seriousness from herself. Quite certainly she didn't know why, precisely at this time, she had to go in search of the child in herself. But intimately personal writing always has to do with keeping oneself intact and with self-discovery; everyone has both the encouragements and the sufferings that are suited to him; so likewise in her room in the evenings, among the numerous notices, in no way clear about herself, she had the satisfaction of seeing her Child in the Evening rise again: frightened, holding tight to the slats of the garden gate. Watching the gypsy family leave the village. Feeling pain, longing, something like a second birth. And saying, finally, "I": I am different.

Some people who knew her then said she had no sense of reality. But the fact is: she couldn't manage money. She smoked, bought expensive soap, and could sit, utterly senselessly, in one of the new HO restaurants and eat ten marks' worth of sauté potatoes and brawn: she would snort with delight. Then, if she was feeling quite mad, she would drink wine; and she wasn't choosy about the company she kept, if company was what she wanted. She questioned everyone, stopped his talk if he got off the subject—I don't want your construction of them, my friend, only the facts, only the true reality, real life. Hungering for reality, she sat in the seminars, insatiable in her appetite for what professors might say about books, saw the poets of past time sink in serried ranks back into the grave, since they weren't adequate, not for us. Cold-bloodedly we abandoned them to their imperfection and moved on. Christa T., who could be assailed by feelings of love and reverence, pulled them out again when evening came and she stayed behind in the seminar library alone. The voices, which no longer argued during the daytime—

for the violent arguments of earlier years had yielded to unanimity, monologues were delivered, based always on the same textbook—these voices came to life for her again at night. The power of facts, in which we believed . . . But what is power? What are facts? And doesn't thinking create facts? Or prepare the way for them? *The pilot who dropped the bomb on Hiroshima,* she wrote in the margin of one notebook, *has been taken to a madhouse.*

She began her walk home. In front of a flower shop in the center of the city a dozen people were standing and waiting silently for the short midnight flowering of a rare and brightly lit orchid. Silently Christa T. joined them. Then she walked home, comforted and much divided in her mind.

Later she couldn't remember how she reached her room and got into bed. She overslept, woke up at noon, and had missed the seminar at which she was due to read a paper. She walked to the window and the snow in the yard was reduced now to a few small islands. Soon, she thought, happy for no reason, it'll be time again for this ornamental stonework to be washed. She laughed and sang, went into Frau Schmidt's kitchen and convinced her that she simply had to take a bath, though it was the middle of the week. Frau Schmidt acquiesced with a sigh—but don't fill it all the way up! —Christa T., laughing still, let the water come right to the top. Then she put on clean clothes and bought, with the last of her money, the expensive bird book she'd wanted for a long time. She sat in her torn leather chair and quietly looked at it. Tomorrow she'd think of all kinds of excuses; she was confident that she'd have convincing ones ready when the time came.

7

I have discovered a new joy in the big city
High on a roof, the city underfoot;
Cocooned in dusk the ocean of the houses,
And slender eastern towers flash a salute.

Across the green and clean cool of the sky
Still shoot these arcs and loops the swallow dares.
From every house a wave of radiance breaks,
And a black turmoil fills the thoroughfares.

I stand and want to sing a song to myself.
The breeze brings fragrance from the lime-tree blooms.
How pleasant it would be to spend the whole night
    here.—
I climb downstairs to dark cemetery rooms.

Twelve or thirteen years still ahead of her. Ought one to wish that she'd found the formula for herself sooner? Would she have become clearheaded about herself? Would the tension have decreased? Would the vibrations have leveled off, between her effortless happy soarings and her terrible downward plunges? I really don't know . . .

She thought that one should see life in all its colors. But, subject as I am to the temptation to approve everything that happened to her or through her, I place this poem of hers before me when I feel myself wanting to get angry. A loose page, one that survived, though it wasn't meant to, one might suppose. The lost pages we know nothing about, and that was intended. Nobody saw this one during her lifetime. It's not hard to guess why. She had good literary judgment. Naturally she'd have smiled at the rhymes, she'd have rejected phrases like "ocean of the houses" and "wave of radiance," and she'd have found the "fragrance from the lime-tree blooms" feeble. But she wouldn't have been averse to the simplicity of the whole, the tone of true feeling. Nothing could be more touching than the period at the end of the stanzas. Four periods in the last, and between the third and fourth lines the dash: between the wish and the suppression of it, between longing and its rebuttal. *How pleasant it would be to spend the whole night here.—I climb downstairs to dark cemetery rooms.*

Coincidence? A promise? Clumsily she had worked this up now from the raw material; and didn't it become hereafter a constant spur? Twelve lines, faded ink on a loose sheet of paper, destined to be lost, but not lost.

She drifted. Another thirteen years. Four successive addresses. Two jobs. A husband, three children. A journey. Sicknesses, landscapes. A few people keep in touch, she comes to know a few others. There's time enough for that. But she hadn't got much time. Yet how can one say that with certainty?

Fortunately life propels even the actions in novels, but

only because of a strange inconsistency of the soul. A romance from her student years: Kostia, as she called him. Kostia, or The Question of Aesthetics.

The pattern shimmers through again.

What does the world need to become perfect? First of all, and for quite a long time, it needs perfect love. Even if only for the sake of our memories, for which one occasionally does have to provide, and even if, at first anyway, it's only for the sake of appearances. Who's talking of love? Love is what one hides, love shuts one up in oneself like an evil sickness; but these two, you can hardly help smiling when you see them together. But you can also stand aside, for the amusement, and let them have their talk; they can't get enough of it. And it really doesn't matter. Just catch Kostia's indecisive look, folks; he's not up to it, he'd better watch out for himself. He is, to be sure, a bit too handsome.

And even if at first it was only a question of looking. She couldn't keep her eyes off him. When he was sitting beside her, he wasn't allowed to turn his head; she growled, wanted to see his profile. So he sat quite still; yet they both must have known that it was all a misunderstanding, and equally so to suppose that we exist in order to be happy. Suchlike solemnities guided her, for it mustn't become a serious affair. We're not going to be pushed, that's agreed, and least of all by ourselves. What concern is it of yours if I love you? Just sit still, beside me, let me look at you, and don't turn your head away, or I'll growl. I won't force you. We'll go along facing in the same direction.

He wasn't all that ingenuous, but he played the game. A pretty game, an exercise for times when one was floating in mid-air, right on the edge of reality. To make the air tremble and to avoid real contact. Bridle one's feelings. What if one doesn't feel anything? Yet feel she did, still smiling; she was in the toils. Even as she gazed, her senses were awakened, the adventure occurred, the strangest of her loves, the least physical. But the pattern shimmers through:

self-abandonment, whatever the consequences. Lack of foresight and restraint. Experience, down to the darkest dregs. A game, but the stakes were high.

I've seen through you, he says one day, I can see your act. Then she knows that he's afraid to confront himself, to see through his own vanity act, which she loves, yes, loves, and which she can't lose, so she laughs: What concern is it of yours, my playing? And so she gave back to him his levity, irresponsibility, the guarantee of his faultlessness, which he needed. His morality as a weapon, his chastity as a shield, because the whole world is a threat to him, with its infinity of colors, forms, and savors, which he can't endure. But she, weaponless, exposed, held out; smiling and playing and wounded by love.

Bettina and Annette, he says, nobody goes by these romantic names any more. Didn't you know?

What does that mean? she asks him.

That you're out of date.

Yes, she says. Perhaps I am. Then I shan't live long. But you, my dear Kostia, you'll grow very old, and that's not meant to be a reproach. You can laugh; but so can I. Once I asked someone three questions, three test questions. He answered one of them correctly, the second not at all, and the third answer was wrong. That's the best one can hope for. He kept using the word "completely"; it always made me wonder.

They go to the new artificial lake together, and he's lying on the beach beside her, she can talk to him as to herself: amazing to think what's been made of it. They swim and go out in a rowboat, lie on their backs, close their eyes, the blue is unendurable and puts an end to the play-acting. Surely he must know that daylight means just this, that it admits of no mistakes. He doesn't say anything. He looks on, while the silence grows more and more intense, till it reaches breaking point. Then he props himself on his elbow and recites: *An einem Tag im schönen Mond September* . . . The whole ballad of a certain Marie A., in hushed

62

tones, with a smile which knows what it's doing and which asks to be forgiven, asks you to understand that it can't help itself.

But you, she says, when you've forgotten my face, you'll know that you recited this poem to her, in a certain place, on a blue day in September. And the poet you thought of, long ago he slept with all your girls for you, with me too, ah Kostia . . . You've seen and done it all, but only in your books; reality could only defile you. But I have to try everything out first, otherwise I don't know anything.

With his face close to hers, she says: Ah, Kostia. When Marie A. crossed your path she was just a depraved woman, nothing more. So you made a detour around her. But she exists; she always exists in reality before she gets into a poem, and before you can admire her in peace . . . You're a prude, she says, for she wants to hurt him too. But he feels appropriately guilty and broad-minded and he keeps saying: I know, I know.

The one and only girl you'd get up off your backside for, she doesn't exist. You have to invent her. You don't understand the simplest things . . .

I know, he says penitently; and she can tell as she looks at his eyes that scores of poems are running through his mind, with a poem to fit every statement she's made. That he can't stop listening to the poems and measuring her real but imperfect statements by them. One day, she realizes, he'll do a swap between the poems, by then become reality, and the person he'll meet, who'll resemble them all: she's like life itself, he'll think, with surprise and satisfaction.

Ten years later Kostia writes Christa T. a letter. By then she'll be sick; the thought of death will have touched her; but there's still hope, the day spent by the lake is a long way off. She'll read the letter as if it were an old and long-forgotten story; and it will come into my keeping with the rest of her papers. I hope he'll forgive me for reading it. I'd do it again, with forgiveness or without it, with or without any right to do so. Not without a feeling of guilt, not without the wish to pay for intruding. Pay for it with justice, as far as that's possible.

The girl now, who appears as his wife in the letter, did exist, a baby sister, blond, needing protection. Protection, above all, from Christa T. Here too she saw through him from the start. She'd have to be called Inge, blond Inge, a name rich in associations. That's how he introduced her, with a smile that was also rich in associations; and she realized—from now on there'll be the three of us. It was inevitable. She loved him, she was at his mercy. Better a clean break than so many small painful retreats: baby sister, she said softly, and for the first time she saw in his eyes something like admiration. The reason why this later became too much for her can be supposed with a high degree of probability, so I have no hesitation in displaying it here as true and real. Kostia's letter alludes, with due tact, to what occurred (or however one wants to put it); and Christa T.'s diary is her own witness. But the events left different traces in each; the secret manipulations and evasions of memory are shown in different ways, in each the rapid and dangerous workings of oblivion take a different course. Accordingly, one can exaggerate the traces or fail to find any, depending on which source you trust. These would be, as far as I can see, the objections which might be raised against my own method; and it would be senseless to defend the method against them. Unless . . . But then there's always an "unless."

It didn't happen the way one can tell it; but if one can tell it as it was, then one wasn't in on it, or it all happened so long ago that candor comes too easily. In order to make the story tellable, one has to separate and put into sequence events which in reality were so entangled as to be inexplicable . . . As far as I can see, this was always the case with Christa T. She was never capable of keeping apart things that didn't belong together: the person and the cause he supports, nocturnal unlimited dreams and limited daylight

64

actions, thoughts and feelings. People told her that, to say the least, she was naïve. This is what Frau Mrosow told her, the headmistress at the school where we took our practical training. She stood in the teachers' room by the window, Kostia was there, but keeping in the background.

It all had to do with Günter; it was a silly affair, at least Kostia called it silly ten years later in his letter to Christa T. Frau Mrosow, he wrote, had for certain reasons galloped off like an old circus horse at the sound of the trumpet, and nobody had been able to do anything about it. But one must needs know what Christa T. naturally knew: that Kostia and Günter had been friends ever since their schooldays and childhood together in the region around Chemnitz.

But we can't approach the story from this angle. For it was, I now realize, a real short story, with introduction, main episode, climax, turning point, and rapid close, with a theme—*Love and Intrigue*—only we didn't see it at the time because we were in the middle of it. Because it has become tellable it seems now like a thing of the past . . .

Anyway: love was Günter's undoing. When we saw Kostia with blond Inge we naturally thought there couldn't have been anything serious between her and Günter; and this was enough to put our minds at rest, for we were convinced that love was contrary to Günter's nature. I don't know how it generally is with love—Günter has never married, to this day—but blond Inge didn't seem to be contrary to his nature. Then along came Kostia and took her away with him in passing, as a third to add to a couple which, strange or not, was already going steady. All this a classic pattern, but God knows what examples Kostia had in mind. Günter, however, took it hard, even if one didn't notice much beyond his becoming a hint more rigid and principled. But he must have been driven to distraction. Yet Kostia told Christa T. to her face that this wasn't the case at all, by the window in the teachers' room, in Frau Mrosow's presence. He lost his head, said Christa T., and I think you know why. Kostia said nothing more and Frau Mrosow, who followed attentively everything Kostia did or felt, came out with her statement: You're naïve, to say the least.

We'd all been sitting there, Kostia too, and blond Inge, and Christa T., when Günter gave his test class in the big auditorium. We sometimes envy the ancients their grand opportunities, speeches in the forum, "Yet Brutus is an honorable man," above all the duel, which was part and parcel of the great world of old: "I do not desire gratitude, madame!" (and he left her that very hour). The grand opportunities come our way, but we don't grasp them, or we let them pass—never do we entrust ourselves to them. Günter had never done so either, which is understandable: what was a test class, compared with Mark Antony's speech in the forum? What was Kostia, compared with Brutus, what were Grade 11 in the Pestalozzi High School and Günter's fellow trainees compared with the assembled citizens of Rome? Günter had planned the course of his hour exactly according to Frau Mrosow's specifications. The students too seemed to know these specifications. In any case they unresistingly and willingly played the question-and-answer game which would infallibly lead to the hour's main objective: demonstrate the superiority of social motives over personal ones as exemplified by Ferdinand's conduct in Schiller's play *Love and Intrigue*.

Günter never got that far.

Later we couldn't remember exactly at what point it began. Perhaps he'd been irritated by that pretty brown-eyed girl who, without batting an eyelid, told him she found the heroine Luise rather extravagant; in a word, *bourgeoise:* unhappy love, in the New Society, was no longer any reason for killing oneself. All the students agreed: we have made progress. This was probably the turning point, and from here things went rapidly downhill. Günter's great moment had come; he seized his opportunity. We all saw his fall, and he saw it too, while his oration confused the students so much they didn't know any more what to believe, and Frau

66

Mrosow was so shocked she was trembling all over—but Günter made no attempt to go back again. He knew what he was doing; he didn't wait for the evaluation of the class, he grabbed his books as the bell rang and he left the auditorium.

That was what brought Christa T. into the teachers' room where Frau Mrosow and Kostia were already standing together. As Christa T. came in, they sprang apart. Frau Mrosow, as everyone knew, hung on Kostia's every word and Kostia himself made the best jokes about it, until nobody found it amusing any more to ridicule an unmarried woman who had a life behind her that was beyond anything we could imagine, who had endured trials which to us seemed legendary. We also had to hold our tongues when she said: You're naïve, to say the least.

But Günter was to be judged as an example, not as Günter: as an example of what happens to a man who falls under the spell of subjectivism. And that's what was done: Günter the man and Günter the case of subjectivism were kept distinct, and Frau Mrosow was the first person who, after the meeting, after all the hands had been raised—mine too, and Christa T.'s, Kostia's also, and blond Inge's—Frau Mrosow was the first person to go up to Günter, shake him by the hand, and even rest a hand on his shoulder. He stayed rigid enough, but he stayed.

So much for the action, and doing justice to the facts. But it isn't the truth. The truth can now be told, and, truly, Kostia wrote it in this letter to Christa T., which I've read: Sometimes, he wrote, everything speaks against one, and one has no defense; and yet one isn't guilty. At least not in the way the others think. —Kostia wasn't meaning Günter but himself. Now, after ten years, Christa T. would have thought him right: by the time Günter was being evaluated, Kostia was no longer guilty. For while Günter had been speaking for his love, as a matter of life and death, Kostia had begun really to love blond Inge; and so Kostia couldn't get his mouth open to admit: Yes, I took her from him, just for fun, and he lost his head. But it wasn't fun, it wasn't a miscalculation, it was fate playing the game, and Günter never chafed against Kostia's silence. Kostia stood there, like a coward, and that's what we thought he was. I'd still be thinking so today if I hadn't read his letter and seen this statement in it: Inge, my wife, has been sick for many years. Things didn't go for me as they should have done. —But the tone of the letter shows that he had no regrets.

I don't know how much Christa T. saw in that test class. I do know that she said goodbye to Kostia that same day, under a lime tree in front of the school. He played the mocking cynic once again: "Under this tree we part, it would seem; Our love was just a beautiful dream . . ." And write that down, he said, write it all down—that's what you want, isn't it? They went their separate ways, and there was even some background music for their parting. From a window came the song: "Now summer comes into the land, Be off with you and your false mind . . ."

You didn't want it so.

The song, which fitted the situation so repulsively, ends of course with a new love.

You're so pale, says Frau Schmidt, when Christa T. comes home after the meeting that night. I hope you're not getting sick. Frau Schmidt likes to go to emotional films; but real pains of the soul horrify her. So what's she to do, when her lodger shuts herself in her room and won't eat or drink anything?

But before that, on the same evening, Christa T. wrote a letter to her sister.

8

When, if not now?

That is how it starts, the letter I'd have liked to suppress, since it wasn't sent, and nobody knows of its existence apart from her and me. So only I do. The very next morning there began what Frau Schmidt respectfully called her "sickness": sitting around, shut in her room, for two days, with hardly more than a piece of bread to eat, until the young man came, no, not the handsome young gentleman but the other, with the freckles, she was just able to whisper a few words to him in the corridor, he was very polite, even to me a simple woman, then he went into her room, and for a long time all you could hear was him talking to her. Until the young lady began to cry, so you could breathe a sigh of relief, see? And the next day he took her to the station.

The letter stayed in her diary.

I didn't really notice that she vanished suddenly, long before the start of the summer vacation, and she didn't write or anything. But it says in the letter that she wanted to die, wanted nothing but that. How could a person whom one saw almost every day suddenly have the idea of dying?

I must unfortunately include this letter, because people usually don't believe that letters like this get written. I'm not inventing it; but I shall shorten it and preserve only the essentials.

Dear sister, Christa T. wrote, in summer 1953. When, if not now?

You know how it is: the time passes quickly, but it passes us by. This breathlessness, or this inability to draw a deep breath. As if whole areas of the lungs have been out of action for an eternity. When that is so, can one go on living?

What presumption: to think one could haul oneself up out of the swamp by one's own bootstraps. Believe me, one doesn't change; one remains everlastingly out of it, unfit for life. Intelligent, yes. Too soft; all the fruitless ponderings; a scrupulous *petite bourgeoise* . . .

You'll certainly remember what we used to say when one of us was feeling forlorn: When, if not now? When should one live, if not in the time that's given to one? It always helped. But now—if only I could tell you how it is . . . The whole world like a wall facing me. I fumble over the stones: no gaps. Why should I go on deluding myself: there's no gap for me to live in. It's my own fault. It's me, I'm simply not determined enough. Yet how simple and natural everything seemed when I first read about it in the books.

I don't know what I'm living for. Can you see what that means? I know what's wrong with me, but it's still me, and I can't wrench it out of myself! Yet I can: I know one way to be rid of the whole business once and for all . . . I can't stop thinking about it.

Coldness in everything. It comes from a long way off; it gets into everything. One must get out of the way before it reaches the core. If it does that, one won't feel even the coldness any more. Do you see what I mean?

People, yes. I'm not a recluse. You know me. But I won't let anything force me; there has got to be something that makes me want to be with them. And then I also have to be alone, or I'm miserable. I want to work. You know—with others, for others. But as far as I can see my only possible kind of activity is in writing; it's not direct. I have to be able to grapple with things quietly, contemplating them . . . All of which makes no difference; the contradiction can't be resolved—none of this makes any difference to my deep sense of concurring with these times of ours and of belonging in them.

But then the next blow—if only you knew how little it takes for anything to be a blow to me!—might fling me up on the beach. Then I won't be able to find my way back on my own. I wouldn't want to live among a lot of other stranded people; that's the one thing I do know with any certainty. The other way is more honorable and more honest. And it shows more strength.

Anything rather than be a burden to the others, who'll carry on, who are right, because they're stronger, who can't look back, because they haven't got the time.

If I had a child, she wrote.

Here the letter breaks off.

And now people won't be asking any more why I wanted to suppress it.

I ask myself.

Because people won't want to read it? I'd understand that. Certainly, too, one can be silent from strength. But there are scars which only give pain when one has to go on growing. Should one keep quiet because one's afraid of the pain?

Yet why didn't I notice that she'd disappeared? What can have been on our minds that summer of 1953?

Yes, she knew about temptations. And she was tempted, at that time, to go. She wasn't able to doubt the world, so all that was left was to doubt herself. Fear: she couldn't live in a world of fear. The inevitability of things in the world as it is: that frightened her. So she shifted across to symbols, and an almost wordless lament: "A child . . ." The living can come later. Ah, to be strong. To hold out. To survive . . .

I'd gladly have left out the letter, or at least made it gentler; but what good would that have done me, seeing that I knew it? So it ended up, as of its own accord, in its right place. My defensiveness hasn't disappeared but has stood to one side. So, unexpectedly, this is the point at which to get the better of it.

One can always say that it had to do with her sickness. The death wish as sickness. Neurosis as deficient capacity to adapt oneself to existing circumstances. That's what the doctor said when he wrote the medical certificate for the university authorities. Best thing for you, Miss T., would be to come to me for therapy. You'd have to realize what's involved. With your intelligence . . . You'll learn to adapt.

Christa T. sent the certificate to the dean's office and never saw the doctor again. She went back to the village. She put a pile of books on the left hand side of the table; she looked to see if the view was the same, seventeen poplars, a hand's width higher than four years ago. At eye level she tacked on the wall a day-by-day schedule of work: her days were to have a framework and she'd keep to it.

At night she has dreams. She glides into sleep as if descending in a cage to the sea floor, only the water becomes brighter, not darker, and finally bright as day, like liquid air. One gives a kick and is floating. It's too beautiful to be sleep. She decides, while still asleep: I'm not sleeping. To float like this isn't surprising if one has wanted it for so long. Whatever happens is true. Kostia, there he is; everything connects. We're drifting toward one another; look, no hands. As we always wanted it to be. But you must look at me now, it's expected, as you know. You'll do it now, any moment. What are you looking at now?

Then she saw the girl. Baby sister, she thought with tenderness. How blond she is, how vulnerable. Oh, how dangerous in all her vulnerability, so much so that he has to keep looking at her. I mustn't come between them, must stand aside. Weep. Can one weep in one's sleep? Yes, I'm sleeping, and I can wake, and I cannot wake, though I've forgotten the most important thing—what was it? To bolt the door, that's it. So pain can't come in. But it's coming in; all this liquid air is really pain. I'm asleep; and whatever happens is true.

But she wasn't made for self-surrender, even though she did have the capacity to be hurt. She was also resilient, with a power to come to the surface again. To find a foothold, inch by inch. The first thing is to make certain of the powers that one still has left, in spite of everything. The poplars, behind which every day the sun sets, whether I watch it or not, whether it pleases me or hurts me. And here are the cherries again, and there's the pond. The frogs when evening comes. Travel miles across country on a bicycle. Stand by the fences and talk with people. Do something, work with my hands, so that I can see what I'm doing: mend the bench that's here and on which my children will sit. Dig the flower bed, pull the weeds out of the strawberry patch. *Senses, dear senses.*

She hardly gives any signs of life to the outside world. *All letter writing is such an effort.* A creature who lives by her eyes, she tells herself: Why can't the powers of reason see, hear, smell, taste, touch? Why this falling apart in two halves? If only I had a job that would enable me to grasp with both hands what I've made or done. It must be wonderful to work with wood. Also with water.

In her most valiant moments she even goes so far as not to reject herself any more: *My thinking is more darkly mixed with sensations, curious. Does that mean it's wrong?* But then, at the slightest sign of failure, a terrible relapse: *How thin it is, the surface I'm walking on. How long can it hold?*

She doesn't ask anyone for help. She fights with herself for herself, and sees no antagonist but herself. She may have been right, almost. She knows now: this may have been just the prelude, now things are getting serious. This feeling reaches us in thrusts: the first thrust seemed to knock her over, but appearances were deceptive.

Learn to adapt oneself! And if it wasn't me who had to do the adapting? —Yet she wouldn't go that far.

An ordinary summer, which mustn't be lost. She won't have many more summers; we have no right to deprive her of this one. She herself, one can be certain, wouldn't have wanted to give this one up. So shouldn't we be sure to share in it today? She saw no reason to draw attention to herself; also no possibility of doing so, I'd suppose. We'd got used to noticing no signs but the strongest ones. There had to be screaming or dying or shooting. Today, though the times are no quieter, we tend more to see a sadness which is only in the eyes, or a joy—by the way a person walks. How she runs, Christa T., after the huge white and red ball that the wind is driving across the beach, how she reaches it, laughs aloud, grabs it, brings it back to her small daughter, under our gaze, which she feels and to which she responds with a side glance, in no doubt as to our admiration. Justus, her husband, walks up to her, runs his hand through her hair, pulls her head back, hi Krischan! She laughs and shakes herself. And all the people along the beach can see her practicing How to Take Big Strides with her little Anna, using as a background, brown and slim as she is, the whole sea which is foaming slightly and the pale sky overhead. Hi, Justus! she shouts.

Hi, Krischan.

Yes, she tells us. Living by the sea!

During the last months, Justus says, she must often have thought of this damned spook man she got mixed up with at that time. He's supposed to have told her: You'll die young. It stuck in her like a hook; there wasn't anything you could do about it.

But perhaps I'd find something about it in her papers, which he was going to give me. For him, he said, it was still too soon to look at them.

For me, too, I had to admit. I began to read, after Justus had left, and didn't stop reading the whole day; and when I'd finished I started all over again, notebook by notebook, jotting by jotting, page by page of manuscript, in the order in which they'd been written. And while doing so I compared every statement with my own memories. Utterly discouraged, I wanted to give up my idea entirely and, as was most natural, let sadness do as it pleased.

Only by now I wasn't free to do so, as I've already said. It can be a rare stroke of fortune to come upon the unknown writings of a person long past, a person of whom posterity is ignorant. To have around one's neck the legacy of a person who—if only everything had been all right—was still alive, this seemed to me at that time a double misfortune, not one that was exactly illuminated by the double meaning of the expression "to acquit oneself." I acquit myself of her, I push her away, relentlessly she's assimilated into the name I've given her, Christa T., while all the time I must cope with the bitter fact that life, after all, is life and paper is only paper, a feeble imprint. Who wouldn't find that depressing?

But we must shake off the sadness and take her and place her before us, though she may be faded, a figure from days long past, and we must have the confidence to be amazed that she ever did exist. So we'll accept them, the yellowing pages of her writings: what time can't do we shall entrust to our thoughts. For in thought we've been watching her a long while now, seeing her tossed around, moving toward a goal which stings her, though she's still resisting its pull. But we, watching, push our underlip out, for we can see what her purpose is and what she's certain to do—one always does arrange for oneself this sort of irrational purpose, only don't ask how, don't ask what pretexts one gives oneself: at all events, we find her plan dubious. All very well to say "plan," but in fact there's no more than a rumor in the villages around. The rumor says that a man has settled in Niegendorf and he has second sight. Snort mildly and go on my way, but how irritating that this rumor should crop up just now, of all times, and reach me, of all people. What do you mean? You wouldn't possibly . . . ?

It wasn't a question of wanting to. Simply that one has been feeling, during these past weeks—how should one put it?—weak, a little susceptible to the supernatural. A relapse, she tells herself. Regressive—well, and . . . ?

Then she heard—as one does get to hear what concerns one—that a small group of people was getting together. A troupe of pilgrims, she says to Frau Kröger, but Frau Kröger doesn't understand: the sudden death of a woman, for whom the spook man in Niegendorf—they called him the General—had prophesied an accident, has raised his prestige considerably. The time has come to go and visit him, troublesome and burdensome though it may be.

Is there still a seat, Christa T. asks, casually enough. If so, I'll come. A chance in a lifetime, to see something like that. She was giving herself an excuse.

The old panel truck left at screech of dawn. Grandpa Fuchs, who has an incurable disease. Frau Kröger, too, perhaps she'll find out something about her husband, who's been missing since the war. Skinny Fräulein Feensen, a few weeks overdue and only a wizard can find her a bridegroom. A few more similar people. They're wondering a bit, but not too much. Why's the teacher going to see the General? She's not sick or we'd know about it. Unhappy in love? Or her father's sickness? He's fading fast, and they say she loves him so. Frau Kröger gives a sigh. Not every Christian shows the cross she bears.

The county seat. If anyone wants to get off now, this is it, ladies. Said that to me, he did. I know Grandpa Fuchs. Doesn't seem to mind if I play deaf. Looks like everyone wants to have me around. Oh, well. I don't believe any of it, says Frau Kröger. *Ick ook nich.* Neither do I. So that's that.

Then come the unknown villages, Gören, Koserow. And the place, too, where the gas mask is lying in the forest, rotted, we mentioned it earlier, when this moment was far into the future, but now it has arrived. She thinks, no, she sees, as if a veil had been ripped away from an image long shunned, only this time she sees from a standpoint outside the action, her munitions truck standing in the snow-storm, herself sitting in it, and a few yards away a little mound, the bundle under it, some flesh and bones and some cloth, gradually the snow covers it.

So you're not getting scared now, miss? Frau Kröger, she always comes straight out with it. But who would . . . Anyway, they say he tells the truth.

9

Wat de Generool seggt hett.

And what if she invented him? For if he didn't exist she'd have invented him because she needed him. Yet she hadn't the courage to invent, of which more later. So he did exist, and he enters the scene as a real person; but at once she hides him, as a precaution, removes him with the irony implied in the dialect phrase introducing "what the General said" in her diary.

Please come a little closer, miss.

It wasn't only curiosity coming into the room, not mere credulity, mere willingness to go down on one's knees before the superior gifts of another person: the man, an Austrian, a retired major-general, assisted by a timid young woman in a dirndl costume—he senses this at once.

He offers her a seat, facing the light; that's the way it's

done. He himself, with his back to the window, remains an outline only; this is how all the little tricks begin, confessions and interrogations.

What was her name? Student, unless I'm mistaken. You see? But it's not important. And not studying, at this time of the year? Or does the summer vacation start earlier nowadays, like everything else, it seems? —He laughs. —Oh, well. Everyone needs to run off for a rest now and then.

Even before she has finished looking around the room, spelling out the mottoes on the walls (all of them have to do with the nullity of human powers), eyeing the pewter pots on the shelf, he knows what he has to know.

And having to give him her hand, what's more, she finds it absurd, perhaps it'd be better to go. The General knows what she's feeling, her excitement has conveyed itself to her hand. All right, he says, we shan't need any more of that. Even goes so far as to make fun of the requisites of his art: no tea leaves, no cards . . . But usually he uses both tea leaves and cards, she knows this, and he, searching her eyes, makes a slight movement with his shoulders: The world, miss, wants to be deceived. But you . . . A person with such clearly marked lines on her hand . . . You can go, he says to the timid young woman.

Your father, miss, works in one of the intellectual professions, unless I'm quite mistaken? A good father. Good mind, and clever with his hands as well. Is he still living? Yes. Even though, as you certainly realize, a human life has its limits. . . Two other children, I see. Only one sister? You love her very much, it's quite clear. As for the other—I must ask you to remember that not only born and living persons exist in the world to which I'm obliged to refer.

Then she thinks: the miscarriage. They tried to keep it secret, but I always suspected it.

The General is satisfied.

And do you know, miss, that the moon's rhythm is very important for you? That your attraction to the southeast line comes from this? Well, perhaps it hasn't been all that noticeable yet, you're still young. Later, when you settle in a city, like, let's say, well, Dresden, then you'll remember what I said, I expect . . .

The stars, yes . . . Venus and Saturn are very close. Venus, love, also tenderness, is always there. But no cause for alarm: I can see a wide circle of stars scattered around you. Many and various things hidden and revealed in it, rich talents, most various interests . . .

Here he was showing insights achieved by psychic affinity: riches like these can sometimes be a burden, as everyone knows.

Of course, of course she invented the General; I must say this here, and put my mind at rest about it: she must have invented him, the day after that séance, back in her room, alone, with a view over the seventeen poplars, her diary in front of her on the table: she invented him with the best of intentions—to be accurate, to be objective, writing down what he said, without once interrupting him, even when he embarrassed her: could one be more just? So she does him justice, in the way anyone would—she extracts the real substance from the stuff and hardly mentions the rest, the abstruse side of it, the errors, my God, yes, the stupid and silly side of it.

I take the liberty of correcting her and invent my own general for myself. To do justice, as anyone would. What next?

You'll soon be taking an examination, her general says. You won't do very brilliantly, as I expect you know. Moderately well, one might say, if one didn't know that your range of intelligence and memory, still restricted at the moment, will become more extensive. You probably know that a woman is at her best when she's in her late twenties. Your best time, miss, will probably come even later than that.

You must be careful, her general says. The next six months will not be an easy time for you. You're in rather a nervous state. You'll be sick on several occasions. What you're going through now, I venture to call a passing phase of reduced vitality.

Here my general looks her in the face, makes sure, lets her finally shake off the reins; or what is it? Then he sees that he can proceed.

Psychological difficulties, says her general, will always come your way when you have to make decisions.

Christa T., Krischan, there she sits, and she feels that she's thinking: he's right. And the light in which he's placed her doesn't conceal this thought from him, either; he leans back, making himself more comfortable, relaxes his grip on her hand, finally permits himself to fill the gap with some routine hocus-pocus.

In the not too distant future, her general says, you'll be summoned to a funeral. Seems it's an aunt, between sixty and seventy, who's died.

Then he sees: this young lady is eluding him now. It's no good, he's got to use all his concentration, my general.

You think about things too much, her general says, and now his tone becomes rather insistent. If I may give you some advice: get rid of this habit, it's bad for your nerves. Believe me: in three or four years—you'd be twenty-four now, wouldn't you, you see?—Well now, when you're twenty-six or twenty-seven, everything will look different to you. Your constellation shows me clearly that you'll stand out above all your contemporaries. That will become quite obvious later on, as long as you have plenty of confidence in yourself: make straight for your goal, but mind you don't overtax your strength, and avoid extremes: just a little bit of know-how, miss, even you need that . . .

Now she's giving in, I see, and so am I. Perhaps he had, in spite of all the rest, a real interest in human beings; perhaps, in all these weeks, he was the only person to find the right words to soothe her, comfort her . . .

As for love at the moment—am I right in supposing you want to know about this?

She doesn't nod, doesn't shake her head, she blushes in the

clear light to which he has exposed her, and makes a movement, as if to draw her hand away, and the General, who
seems not to have noticed, lets go of her hand.

You like to be in love, her general says—or who is it saying this? You love tenderly and warmly, but your love is
like friendship. That's why you have good friends, you're
sociable, sympathetic toward people. Until this dissatisfac-
tion comes over you—you know what I'm talking about.
Then you become moody, can even repulse people who are
close to you, even people who love you, you know why.
Those are the bad times when everything goes cold, and
they follow the times of great love . . .

Who said this to her? Does she know now why she came
to see him? But how can he possibly have known that?

No, he can't keep it up, our general, if he's forced down
among the concrete details, or takes off into prophecy,
which is, as he must know, part of his function. There
seems to be a man in her life who's trying to encourage her
to get married. Our general advises her to have nothing to
do with this marriage, for it will certainly bring sorrow,
jealousy, interruption of professional progress . . .

Then it's time again for him to take her hand. What are
we to foretell for her in the professional line?

This is what our general asks; pensively he reads her
palm once more. A job in a large institution? It's possible.
Something like a publisher's, I believe . . . A difficult start:
it can't be helped, as you know. And then definitely you'll
get on all right. And more than that: if I'm right, miss,
you'll become well known. I might even say: famous. As I
see it, everything points to something creative here. A book?
Music, perhaps? No, not music. Literary, that's it. Well,
that's all I can tell you. But why do you suppress your wish
to be a lady of leisure now and then? There shouldn't be
any financial difficulty in the way.

How does she suddenly imagine herself now? A long
dress, flowers, admirers? What's up with me? Shall I let
him go on? Go on, General, don't let me stop you.

Probably a doctor, her general says, your future husband. Even a professor, maybe? The most propitious time for you to marry would be six or seven years from now. Love will be the basis of this marriage—well, that goes without saying. And your husband will be seven or eight years older than you. I see two children, healthy. No major events.

Go on, General.

A friend will introduce you. At the opera? At the publisher's? You'll understand: it's not possible to be more precise. But this much: a house outside the city, possibly in the country, it might even be in a park. Life runs its course in a beautiful straight line, keeping all the chances open for you to develop your rich character and your talents, your unusual mixture of romantically poetic gifts with practical ones, pedagogy, teaching . . .

Go on, General, don't forget anything, we want all the embellishments! Shall we have a car? What model? Or shall we have a four-poster bed instead?

Perhaps she shouldn't have let it be felt that she was eluding him once more. For now he takes her hand a last time. Now come his final words, regarding the end of her life.

Then, after all, she closes her diary; and then she brings it out again: at last she has written down the final words and now it looks as if all the previous pages were written only for the sake of this sentence: *Your marriage,* she wrote, *will end with a death. Either the wife's or the husband's. But the children will have left school by then.*

She reads everything through again, including the last sentence. Then at the end she writes two words enclosed in brackets, with a question mark: *So soon?*

Now she finally closes the book.

Ick glöw doar nich an: I don't believe any of it. But it's certainly strange.

End of scene.

She never reread these pages; and, as time passed, the script of her mind came to resemble less and less that of the diary. She didn't win at tombola, nor did she go to the spa for a health cure the following year; and the funeral of the aunt was some time in coming. She doesn't notice it. But an early end has been foretold for her, that she does remember. The only thing he was careful not to say, she'll remember it always: I shall die young.

And she can't help believing it.

Not another murmur about the General.

10

Regressive, we'd have said and shaken our heads; and we'd have been right. She might have told her story to one or two people, tentatively, quietly. If she did so, she'd have seen on all the faces, without exception, this incredulous and pitying smile appear. This I can guarantee; I can still feel the imprint of that smile on my own face.

So she didn't say anything.

The story one has to tell won't be anything important.

So one can just as well write it down. Take the edge off this incurable propensity for writing, simply by giving in to it without taking it seriously. If the trick works, one is saved for the time being. I close my eyes and what do I see in my mind? Nothing important, as I said, and you can tell it's not important because it comes of its own accord, effortlessly, without being forced, no pattern, no significance. A page is quickly torn from a notebook; once again the work schedule isn't followed and you make no progress in the grammar book. A few titles scribbled down, tentatively, as they come, something already worked out in the head, as it turns out, little stories, for later. When, if not now?

"List of titles" is the phrase written on the page, between quotation marks, exactly as reproduced here. And one can use the quotation marks at least to indicate your ironic distance. In the course of time, more than two dozen titles were listed; I've found others on loose scraps of paper. Some I understand, others not. I can't read all the scribbles; she couldn't have even read them herself. Would she have wanted to?

The question is insinuated, it really doesn't belong here. Asked prematurely? Indeed, it's the trickiest question I've been faced with while thinking about Christa T. For when people ask me about this—and they *will* ask, that's for sure —I shan't be able to produce anything: why bring her up at all, people will ask. For that's what I'm doing, there's no denying it.

So they'll force me to talk about success, actual results: did she succeed? But where is this getting me? What testimony shall I be able to give?

Günter occurs to me, Günter with the freckles, *before* his great performance, before love caused his fall and sorrow, yes, sorrow had made him clairvoyant. He always defended Christa T. and he was always angry with her. He may in those days already have admired her as an individual; there are several indications of this; but he couldn't get along with her as a type. He believed too steadfastly that everything in existence had to be useful; and he was tortured by the question why an invention like her had to be necessary —though she had "all the makings," as he himself admitted. Look, he said, when the deadline for a two-semester seminar paper had passed and not one of the group had seen a single line by Christa T.—look, society has helped you to study, and now it wants something of you in return, right? Yes, said Christa T., who always had long talks with Günter, listening to all his proofs and thinking them over thoroughly: Yes, it's right, but it's not good, you know. I'd even say it was—expensive. —What do you mean, Günter asked; you're being facetious.

Yet she wasn't, far from it. She simply felt a powerful inner resistance to paying any price in foreign currency. But she still couldn't believe that her own currency had its own value; and it's true—where could she have found such a belief?

So what testimony can I give? This: that the times were working for her. But time was the one thing she didn't have. Wasn't she told this very early on?

When I got this far, I lost my temper. I've read the list of titles once more. *At the Forester's. Summer Evening. Rick Broders. Jan and Christine. Day by the Sea. The Elde Fields.* —What does it all mean? Try as I might, I can't figure out what's at the back of these titles. My anger, which was complicated, was the healthy fury of a reader bereft of a promised story. And even if I was the only person who'd like to know what it means, this title for instance—*Lieutenant Baer was different*—shouldn't she at least have shown some consideration for me? Perhaps there's no point in being concerned about the anger of one individual; but I thought—unjustly, as it happens—that she should have been concerned about mine. Or she should have torn up the scraps of paper, and left it at that. What justification did she have? She, down there, buried, she, at whose head—this is how one speaks about the dead—the buckthorn bushes grow.

De mortuis . . .

I left it all on the table and went out. I told myself: I'm not going to do it; people can't really expect it of me. How happy I was to have my beautiful anger. I stood in front of a kiosk, read the signs a dozen times. I noticed that I still couldn't get away from the thought that would quench my anger: I thought: she would have done it, all of it.

So unfortunately I had to give up my anger. One shouldn't get angry with the dead. But I was hurt, and I still am. It isn't right, what they say: that only the living can hurt one. But if it was right, what would this other hurt mean?

I was going to talk about success. But success, when it occurs, always has a story attached to it; so does failure, but we're not concerned with that. Success can be genuine or artificial, deserved or stolen, a natural development or something forced . . . But above all it can consist in this or that: in fame, for instance, or in the delayed certainty that one has to do a particular thing and cannot do otherwise.

So I should have to tell, among other things, the story of Christa T.'s success. The thought surprises even me.

A slight bitterness remains after my anger, but it'll pass, soon. Then perhaps I shall see her: see her as she should be and thus as she was. But however long this account of her lasts, it seems to be certain that the moment to see her will only come after it has been completed.

But that will be the moment of freedom and magnanimity, coming of its own accord.

She, Christa T., made a great discovery that summer, not without knowing that she'd done so, but without knowing that it was great. Suddenly she saw something like a link between herself—this life which did strike her as being too ordinary and often even narrow—and these free magnanimous moments. She began to realize that one must create the moments oneself and that she had the means for doing so. There had always been this longing of hers, her particular *Sehnsucht*. *Sehnsucht* comes from *sehen*, to see, and *Sucht* craving. This craving to see, and this was her discovery, accorded with actual things in a simple but irrefutable way.

I don't know whom she might have had in mind, but it seems there was someone there to whom she told this unfinished story—*Malina, the Strawberry:*

When I was thirteen years old I was allowed for the first time to go on a journey with the rest of the family. For a whole year letters had been coming from Uncle Wilhelm—carbon copies, that is, of the letters which he typed in triplicate and sent to all the relatives. Uncle Wilhelm, till recently a prison inspector in Brandenburg, had taken the chance offered by the Führer to officials of junior and intermediate rank: to attain positions much higher than the regular ones established many years back. The eastern regions were calling for able administrators, and Inspector Krause went there to become Chief Inspector with substantive rank and salary in a government office.

The place was Warthegau, a suburb of Kalisch; his address was Litzmannstädterstrasse 2; and the year was 1940.

For two weeks before we left I sat in the garden under the summery lime tree, darning and sewing away at my panties and socks. I was very much looking forward to the trip, and was convinced that you had to take along everything you possessed.

I have only the faintest impression of the journey itself. Roasting summer heat over yellowish green fields, a dull quietness in half-empty compartments of the train. In Kreuz they only glanced at our passports, hardly the right thing to reinforce my illusion, stubbornly disputed by my mother, that I was going to visit a foreign country.

From my Brockhaus encyclopedia, dated 1889—a legacy from my grandfather, and the principal book in my library—I knew that Kalisch was a provincial district in the western part of Russian Poland: "Flat lowland with a westward declivity and insignificant elevations. The climate is moderate and healthy. The population is 80% Polish (mainly Roman Catholic), 10% German (mainly Protestant), 9% Jewish, and, for the rest, Russians and others. The soil is sandy. An important area for sheep farming and the raising of geese, which are exported to Germany. The province has eight districts: Kalisch, Wjelun, Kolo, Konin . . ." and so on.

I recited all this to my mother. How foreign it sounds, she said. But she wouldn't agree that I'd be going to a foreign country. "It's German," she said, "no question of that." But she was interested to hear that "Kalisch, Polish Kalisz, lies in a beautiful valley among three branches of the river Prosna," and that it had "six annual fairs." "Well then," she said, "it won't be such a desolate place after all"; and her mind was put at rest.

At midnight we arrived in Kalisch.

Now one ought to know why she stopped at this point. What was to be the outcome of this Polish strawberry—Malina—for which she had raised the whole magic structure, with Brockhaus 1889, the journey to a foreign country which wasn't any such journey, her mother and herself, talking and replying . . . You asked what testimony I've got. Well: the tone of these pages of hers, for example. She speaks so you can see her.

That's all.

Then somebody must have called her away. There was a visitor. Visitor wanting to see me?

Yes, it was the schoolmaster from the next village, and how kind of him to come. Even if she didn't know what it might mean, what the look in his eyes meant, apart from neighborly friendliness. A sort of signal, which anticipated a recognition; but it found no echo in her.

Her mother sent them into the jasmine arbor and brought some cider; later, also, the moon rose. At first his talk is rather forced, and she can't think why. He has heard that she's sick, or something, and had to come and see her. He has handsome brown eyes to see with, she can't help thinking; his candor and calmness make her feel good, too—where can she have met him before? Good mind, clear judgment, an active and warmhearted attitude to life. She'd like to go to his school as a student. He at once endorses her thoughts by starting to talk about his students, of whom several are still known to her, so she becomes attentive, asks questions, explains, contradicts, wonders. Yes, he says at one point, we're all four years older than we were.

She agrees and laughs. Not a particularly bright remark, but not an untrue one either.

Then her father comes, it has been a good day for him, the first for a long time, without any of these pains, almost without any of his breathlessness; he's sure he'll be all right, sitting beside them in a blanket. The talk about school stimulates him and he talks about his own schooldays, his years in a teachers' college, his attempts to break away, and how he finally found his place. How different, Christa T. thinks, and at the same time what similarities! Her father won't often talk with her this way again, she knows, and he knows it too. He gets on well with his young colleague from the next village; they start talking shop, and suddenly Christa T. hears the young man say: I agree with you completely!

Completely. This finally gives her the jolt she should have felt at the start; and it explains his meaningful looks and the ambiguity of his replies. Now she notices, too, that he's wearing the same old gray zip jacket. It's a good one, more durable than one small feeling.

And yet: God, how can one forget a thing like that?

She likes him and doesn't like him.

When in the night she's thinking of this—of all the things that happen, the things one forgets, forgetting what one liked and didn't like—suddenly all her sadness and despair dissolve and she's consoled. Well, well, she thinks with amazement. Well, well.

For the first time she falls asleep quickly, doesn't wake too early, but on waking feels fresh and remembers what she has dreamed. She was standing by the fence, as long ago; the schoolteacher from the next village came riding past, wearing his gray jacket, and she stuffed his pockets full of cherries, only they were green ones, but that didn't seem to bother either of them. Then it wasn't him any more but Kostia, she gave him big handfuls of cherries, and suddenly twilight came, it was night, the moon was in the sky. Then the man looked at her—for it wasn't Kostia any more but a stranger, and he said kindly: You see? That's how it always is.

All next day she repeated this phrase to herself and couldn't help laughing. That's how it always is, that's how it always is—why is that so consoling? She didn't worry about not knowing who the stranger was.

At noon her sister arrived on her bicycle and it occurred to her that the summer vacation had begun. They bicycled together to the meadows by the dike, lay in the grass and talked about everything that can be talked about. The other thing, Malina the strawberry—that too had now begun as well, in secret. But how often she would deny it still, how often deeply doubt it.

It was never completed.

II

I can only say: she carried it along with her.

For the way she was to take wasn't free from contrary influences, and so it was long and arduous, like many of the ways of our generation. But it was a way, a direction had been taken; what was to come had now announced itself, had, after long labor, even shown what shape it would have to take: its reality and its arduousness could be told incontestably from the force of her unrest, as one can tell from the deflection of a needle the tension that's pulling at it.

She must now consolidate her courage to be herself; the summer isn't over. She no longer proceeds at random. The initiative is taken not by the next best thing to come along but by herself working to an open or secret plan. *I find the nineteenth century admirable from a literary point of view.* She reads Raabe, Keller, Storm, clings to sobriety, descends, without knowing it, into the world of small things. Definite processes, sharply outlined, visible in the round, down to the finest ramifications of feeling, which remain, all the same, uncomplex. Her other love, almost a vice—complicatedness, multisignificance, subtlety, the end-of-an-epoch feelings, Thomas Mann—this now takes second place. What she notes for her own use are stories which she has got other people to tell her, life stories, traditional and manageable matters, as if she mistrusted imagination profoundly, as if imagination were a source of possible error. Firm clear outlines, nothing dissolved in feeling, nothing refracted by the play of thought. *Make the writing hard,* she demands of herself, *dry humor, sharp eye, distinguish between genuine feeling and sentimentality, beware of imitations! Precision!* I decipher these words in the margin of an unfinished manuscript: *Gottfried Keller: one should be able to read stories over and over again.*

She wouldn't have gone so far as to write: my stories.

One asks, all the same, if it might not have helped to live with illusion somewhat longer. One might do so, at least, until the disproportion between one's demands on oneself and one's actual powers ceases to be a source of oppression. Gradually increase the disillusionment, so that one isn't floored by the first unmitigated attack of what people call insight.

Now, in any case, she wants to find out what particular work she'll have to do. For this very reason she goes, when the new academic year has begun and she has returned to the city—how remote they are, the defeats which drove her away, how comical and inept the cautiously sympathetic look on Frau Schmidt's face—she goes before anyone else does, as if something might be snatched from her, straight to her professor, and makes certain of her thesis topic: the writer, Theodor Storm.

At my request the institute has sent me the thesis, and obligingly indicated that it needn't be returned at once. I know: there it stands—a grayish springback folder with a green calf spine, number 1954/423—stored with hundreds of other theses which the decades have deposited; and only the dry dust of the institute shows any interest in them. The dust soon makes it all the same whether the examiner wrote "Very good" on the last page, as in this case, or just let it pass. And because it's the rule, each student wrote at the very end of his effort the one sentence: *I certify that the foregoing is entirely my own work and that I have used no sources except those cited. Christa T.* The date was May 22, 1954. She had eight years and nine months left. The clock is wound up, don't worry, it's running down. From now on, its ticking shall accompany us. She never showed her work to any of us, and we didn't ask to see it. Probably she had to overcome resistances in herself before she could hand it in to the secretary of the institute—and it was submitted late. Günter reminded her every day as the deadline approached. The "Very good" mark she noted with indifference; she won't ever have reread what she wrote. There wasn't a copy of the thesis among her papers.

So I'm reading it for the first time, anticipating the haughty tone and ready-made, clattering sentences with which in those days we attacked rather than grasped our topics. I didn't anticipate compliant understanding, the confessions, even less the self-questioning and almost undisguised self-portrayal, the eruption of personal problems into the dispassionate inquiry.

Much depends on the right questions being asked at the right time, and she, Christa T., was lucky: the question is ripe for asking—how, if at all, and under what circumstances, can one realize oneself in a work of art.

So it comes about that, as I read, I can hear her speaking. She talks about the mental adventures of her poet, and it doesn't seem to disturb her that a relation is established between him and another person who remains unspecified but who is present. Why did she choose Storm? She says: because his attitude to the world is "predominantly lyrical," and because a nature like his, in a period of cultural inertia and derivativeness, is especially hard put to produce its proper work. So what interests her is the endeavor: she doesn't overrate the work itself, but she does value its having come to be. Not that she defended Storm as a writer of idylls; neither did she attempt to argue that his particular province is a grand poetic realm. What matters is that he really did conquer his realm, against the worst odds.

I can see where he's going, her poet, just as I can hear her speaking. There are several qualities that she finds permeating him—for instance, the *nervous sensitivity*—and by no means does she deplore the *immediacy of the impressions;* she declares her liking for some qualities too: his *integral artistry, which reflects a full humanity.* Others, also, she credits him with: he *rescued poetry from the destruction threatening human personality when it becomes merely marginal to events.* She can't deceive anyone who knows how to read for himself; perhaps, this once, she didn't want to deceive anyone regarding the unrest detectable behind her rigorous and just judgments. She doesn't say "I," of course. Not yet. The subjects are "we" and "one": *Again and again one feels in his poems the horror experienced by an integral human being who loves life passionately and is facing the necessity of death, the threat of nothingness* . . .

She, the writer—*to think that I can only cope with things by writing!*—knows that she herself is threatened and tempted by a hankering for the merely marginal, the small pastoral piece, the particular case, the transparent and simple figure. She knows only too well how to avoid everything ugly. Even if one is resigned, still to generate in oneself courage and energy and try to convey them to the reader . . . This is the direction in which "one" follows him. She lets herself be drawn, too, into the limited world of his characters, *lovable, rich in feelings,* but she does remark that as personalities they are narrowly circumscribed by the repetitive themes of love and family life: *The human relationships are so scant that the flame soon subsides* . . .

"One" has to distance oneself from this, push off, summon all one's courage, even if the courage is directed against oneself: *It is true—the conflicts seize hold of the whole person, force him to his knees and destroy his sense of individuality. But the people do not get on very well together, and they have little to defend themselves with. That, indeed, is their weakness.*

The "indeed" is revealing. That's how one counters objections. That's how one speaks of living persons against whom one cannot help measuring oneself. As if anyone could stop the spate of her talk now. As if anyone could force her to look up and listen to what might now at last be argued against her, and why not before? But the recital of her experiences goes forward, her voice isn't raised, she herself applies the restraint, reprehends herself for the fascination, which was unmistakable: *The conflict between willing something and the inability to do it thrust him into a corner of life* . . .

And she even shows—but where did she obtain it, at that time?—insight into the basis of tragedy, demanding tragedy of her poet rather than his *unhappy personal consciousness.* The tension which swayed his life could have torn him apart. But he avoids *ultimate intellectual consequences* and remains comparatively intact; *he vents all the pain done to his sensitive heart before the conflicts can reach an ultimate intensity and sharpness.*

This in an offended tone. Whom is she putting right? She's not petty when she's severe. The obligation is to end tragically, or to achieve a life task fully. Thus to be happy. Everything in between is weakness.

And then, just when one has ceased to expect it, she does appear in person, undisguised, as "I." One can hardly believe one's ears: what can have prompted her to contrast her own childhood with the poet's? A compulsion to assert herself, after so much self-criticism?

> *I should present here the reaction of a normal reader —my own—to one of Storm's stories, stories by a writer who made a landscape of longing, of Sehnsucht, out of*

97

the quiet places which impressed him deeply in his boy-hood. Similar experiences in my own childhood come to mind. Stalking red deer with the forester in the woods —returning to my grandfather's tree nursery. Far back, enclosed by dense green shrubbery, the bee house with its humming hives on the open side facing the sun; the simple equipment on the wooden wall; Grandfather on the bench telling stories; Grandmother's beloved and beautiful face among the confusion of leaves at the gate in the hedge—part of the unforgotten joy of a village childhood comes to life again. The colors of memory are a greenish gold.

There it is again, the language of her sketches, there her voice is heard again. Yet it will eventually have to stop; the moment is coming when the voice fails, and it can't be interrupted. Some details pass me by, while I anticipate the end. Now the end comes; and unfalteringly the voice speaks these last sentences too:

There are poems and stories by Storm that will not pass away. But they will be understood differently by people who come later, happier people. Less lonely sorrow will flow from them. Rather, an intense feeling for life will be discovered in them, the melancholy of that joy in moments of solitude which even the most serene people always need. Storm's most beautiful writings will be read and loved for a long time, as an image of human beauty created by longing.

The goal of this account of Christa T. was to find her—and to lose her again. To know both and to accept both. To set about it and write the first sentence: the quest for her—in the thought of her. Then sentence by sentence: for months on end not a day spent without her; until there'd be nothing left to do but send her away, again. To withdraw her support, having just made certain of it. Or to be certain of it only then.

The greater part is done.

12

So we celebrated the New Year in our Berlin apartment located between the S-Bahn, Kohlenplatz, and the power station. Christa T. sometimes sailed in, as into a port, for compared with her life the apartment was a steady place. She ate supper with us, played with the child; and she said: I'm going to have five children, and I asked: But who with? She gave a shrug. She sat on the floor and listened to the new records; then we made up her bed in the loggia. But she didn't go to sleep. What's the matter, I asked. Does the S-Bahn disturb you?

Not in the least. I'm counting the trains. The power station has just shot a sheet of fire into the sky. And in spite of it all you've got a nightingale in your garden.

You're hatching something, I said. I still kept thinking that one should keep an eye on her, "take her in hand" as they say. Or at least protect her.

It's very funny, she said, that we've all become something.

Nowadays, I suppose, this feeling calls for an explanation. But first I'll let her go on talking. She went on, or asked: Think—are you really living today, at this very moment? Really living?

Heavens, I said, where's this leading?

Today I'd like to be able to give her question back to her. For she was right, now I come to think of it. We never realized one might some day arrive somewhere and that would be the end of it. That one would be something, and think no more of it. We were traveling, and there was always a little wind behind us, or against us. We aren't anything yet, but we shall be one day; we haven't got it yet, but we shall: that was our formula. The future? The future is going to be Quite Different. Everything in good time. The future, beauty and perfection, we're saving them up, as our reward, to be paid some day, for untiring industry. Then we shall be something, then we shall have something.

But as the future was always thrust along in front of us, and as we saw that it was nothing but the extension of the time that moves with our own movement, and that one can't ever reach it—then we had to start asking: *How* shall we be? *What* shall we have?

Time cannot stop, but one day there'll be no time, unless one stops now: are you really living now, in this very moment, really living?

When, if not now?

During the mornings she works at the school, Christa T., but more of that in a moment. She goes back briefly to her dark, tubelike room, her shabby landlady, takes a rest, insurmountable the possibilities latent in the first few working weeks—then out she goes, every afternoon she explores the city.

Hurried jottings in her reddish-brown notebook. The young women have become surprisingly beautiful. The quick glances exchanged when two of them meet, nowadays, at the train station. They've made it, these young women, walking through the shops after the day's work, or fetching the children from the nursery school; one can see most from their hands, which are strong but not insensitive, they can support their husbands too, if needs be, and who taught them that? She's teaching them, Christa T., equal among equals. Her smile, her walk, her movement when she helps a child who's fallen. The irony with which she makes an obstinate schoolboy see reason. The firmness with which she insists on tidy and honest work. Look, children, let's not slacken off now.

And why not? Because the big ideas never live of their own accord but are fed by our lives. *"Edel sei der Mensch,"* it says in the poem: let man be noble. She shuts the book, a girl at the back of the class is furtively combing her hair. We must have big thoughts about ourselves, or else everything is pointless. That's what the teacher says, doesn't she? Learn it by heart, she says. Comb your hair when you're doing so, if you want, stand at the window waiting for your boyfriend, but the point is to think of the words as your own. *"Denn das unterscheidet ihn . . ."*—that makes him different. Yes, that was a great thought.

She's a riot, the new teacher, she hears one boy say during the morning break, now she even wants us to sweat over these textbook poems, seriously. The other boy simply shrugs: I know it by heart already, he says, easy as that. He pulled a radio transformer out of his pocket: found this, he says, fantastic dump out there, nobody's ever gone over it. Do you think we can use it? —His friend gave a look she'd never seen in the classroom. That afternoon she stayed home, correcting their written homework. She brought the exercise books to me in the evening. —Read them, she said. The best class in the school.

I can remember those essays very well, the topic too—it was one of the regulation topics of those years: Am I too young to contribute to the development of the Socialist society? I read the essays, all twenty-four of them. Yes, I said, there's a new generation every ten years. What should I do,

Christa T. said. I ought to give them all a D. But it's for a competition, and if I do, our school will come off badly. They'll think I'm crazy.

Why get so excited about it? I asked.

Christa T. simply didn't want her class to be telling lies. She talked to her students; she criticized one especially, whom she called Hammurabi:

In glowing colors you describe, she said, what you can do for society as a member of the Youth Association. But as far as I know, you're not even a member.

Hammurabi looked blank.

That's right, I'm not, he said, but I could be, couldn't I?

Almost wordlessly the students taught her about certain rules of the game in practical life. The girl at the back even stopped combing her hair for a moment and told the teacher that nobody could actually force her to be so stupid as to mess up the grades, and a D, if the teacher really wanted to risk that, well, she for one wasn't going to put up with it. And worst of all, the class made it quite clear that they understood the teacher's anger but saw it as the anger of inexperience, the sort of feeling they'd got over long ago.

The school principal was an old man, who has now passed away. When he had listened to Christa T., he sent his secretary to make some coffee. You've got a little time, have you?

As far as I recall, he didn't say a word about the essays.

This man—she told me about him, but I never met him—will have to be invented here. He didn't talk about himself, or he talked exclusively about himself, it depends how you look at it. For he doesn't distinguish between himself and the times. He's a survivor, one of the old crowd, and his days are numbered, he knows it too. Moreover, he's a historian, a convinced materialist, an educated man—the years in prison, he says with a smile, were also part of his education—and he's a passionate teacher—I never want to be anything else.

The girl facing him—for he can only see her as a girl—is

all worked up. For him the scene is nothing new; how many people have sat thus before him: he knows how it will turn out, he knows this type of person. He even thinks, or senses, for a fraction of a second, that he's had all too many scenes of this kind and that he knows all too often how it will turn out, right every time, and that nowadays it's very seldom indeed that anything for him is really new. Well, he knows also what this feeling means. It's certainly not a sign that he's had enough, it's more like wisdom. He smiles. Wisdom, that would crown everything.

What can they actually have talked about, these two, and at that particular moment? Conversation falters when one speaker knows too little and the other knows, or senses, too much. But often he asks himself whether he wouldn't like to be in their shoes, these youngsters, with their smooth brows and bright excitement, working themselves up, good God, about nothing at all. As for the essays, better not waste any words on them. Learn to keep your own thoughts to yourself, it's what makes life livable, laughter too—is that so difficult for them? —He supplies his own answer: as difficult as it was for us.

But here the similarities cease. Yes, he's a bit arrogant, he has to be. His fate won't be repeated, not in these youngsters' lifetime, whether they've deserved to be spared it or not. They'll never fully understand us, that's a fact. A fact that makes one lonely. What can they know?

What can I know, Christa T. thinks. Naturally he finds me comical. Perhaps he's right. We shall never do what he's done.

We shall never agree, thinks this old man; and he knows that agreement can't always be reached. So he's one up on her. Moreover, he views the girl with a trace of prejudice, just as she views him: each has an image of the other, and each knows that the other has this image; I can try to change it, or I can adapt to it. But only the old man knows how difficult it is to change an image. He gives up trying, nowadays, more often than not. She'll learn, too. Something like pity, mixed with envy. Once he too was one of the excitable people. Nothing is left of that but the sense that such people are not the worst sort. And: that they must be checked. He has thought it all out long ago, the examples have been forgotten, but the doctrine has stayed put. They won't have to buy their lives at the price we had to pay—it's a momentary feeling, but the thought to match it is: one can't treat every individual case on its own merits starting from scratch.

The touch of routine doesn't escape Christa T.; but who'd argue that a thing is right because it's part of a routine? So she agrees that at all times, even when it's difficult, one must distinguish between what is essential and what is not. He reads her mind: How often I've been told that!—for he hasn't forgotten how to read people's looks, it has saved his life once or twice, and he still likes the feeling it gives to see through another person.

If only you knew, he thinks, how often that's been said to *me*. Then he can't help smiling, when he notices that nobody has needed to say it to him for quite a long time now —he says it to himself. Often.

But this way we're not making any progress. Do I *want* to? The old man hesitates. —Didn't sleep so well last night, who's going to ask why? Not me, why should I? His self-control returns.

He says, thoughtfully: You want to have everything at once: power and goodness and I don't know what else besides.

He's right, she thinks and she's astonished. It hadn't occurred to her that one shouldn't want to have all those things. Suddenly she understands: that's how it is with him. He has trained himself to want only as much as he can reach by using all his powers. Otherwise he wouldn't be alive today, or he wouldn't be sitting here. There was no more to be said. But the easy sayings—like One's actions should match one's thoughts, or The Integrated Life, or No Compromise, The Truth and Nothing but the Truth—he'd put them all behind him.

The funny thing is, he says, interrupting her thoughts, that life goes on—I couldn't be telling you anything more banal, you'll probably think. But this banality can sometimes be the most important thing of all . . .

So her thoughts come full circle and meet in the midst of the conversation she's having; and we'll leave it at that. As things stand, we can't hope for anything better. He knows too much, but not enough, yet he does have forebodings, which reality will overtake: he can't hope for any more nights made easier by new certainties. So he doesn't know whether he's waiting for certainty or is afraid of it.

Either way, he has no choice but to say nothing of it. This young woman there, ah, with her essays!

As she leaves, Christa T. doesn't know what to think: what, actually, has he said to her? Nothing, to be accurate. Yet there was something, a curious remark at the end: This much is certain, he said, and don't you ever forget it—what we have brought into the world can never be driven out of it.

At first she'll forget this remark; but it comes up again, in its own good time. Now, while she's on her way home, a new feeling is paramount, an odd enough feeling. She's suddenly glad that she has wishes which go beyond herself and beyond the time that I shall see in this life, she tells herself. She'd never thought of it before. She's grateful to that man, the principal, and not in the way that she might have been grateful to the image she had of him. She's grateful to him for her wishes. He helped to pay for them.

Their conversation might have been like this, but I won't insist that it was. We've made for ourselves the most various images of one another; some are so durable that one wants them no different. Perhaps the principal wasn't like this, but he could have been. One can't ask him, he's dead now. But how could one even have asked him when he was alive? How should one know what image he'd have had of himself and which image he'd choose to display? Ten years later. He wouldn't want to clamber back into the mine shaft. For he would have had to go easy on the strength he had left.

It's a striking fact that it needn't have been she, Christa T., sitting in front of him. In this scene she's interchangeable with countless other people her age. Many, but not all. The time was approaching when she'd become different, but we didn't realize this. Until we stood in it up to our necks.

What follows now could have happened to nobody but her. The Toad Story. I hadn't been aware that it had affected her so much. She said little about it, just a few words. Imagine, just recently a boy in my class bit off the head of a toad in my presence. Dreadful, I must have said, ah yes, now I remember: we drafted a letter, as a joke, to our old teacher-training professor, which culminated in the question: What does a young lady teacher do, dear Herr Professor, when in her presence an almost grownup student is overcome by the desire to bite off the head of a common country toad?

I take the whole story from her now with a clear conscience, since she wrote it down, covering twelve pages, and it's not important whether it happened exactly as she described it or not. Let's begin, as she does, with the last evening before the school working-group leaves the village, now that the potato harvest is almost over. We'll begin in the village inn. Christa T. has given her students permission to have a party, and now one can see their heads through the fug of smoke above the tables: Wolfgang, playing chess with the tractor driver; Jörg, trying to play a Beethoven sonata on the out-of-tune piano; Irene, arguing about comics with a village boy. Christa T., the teacher, is sitting with the farm people at the table of honor in the corner, and she's being treated to beer. *It seems to me that when I started I somewhat underestimated my profession and the psychological make-up of my students . . .*

Let's move on to the following day. The misty chill of the early morning, the wet potato plants, the clammy fingers. The last field. It'll be done by midday, if Hammurabi so wishes. Christa T. measures the length of the field with a glance, then she looks at Hammurabi, moves her head back and forth doubtfully—purely tactical moves. Hammurabi hasn't noticed anything, he needs no challenge, he exchanges a look with Wolfgang, gives a whistle, and then the two of them start off, the basket between them. Christa T. is confident they'll have reached the far edge of the field by breakfast time. She stays behind with the girls—sometimes it's wise to let the men steal a victory. The girls beg her to tell them, for laughs, a few more Plattdeutsch proverbs: *Wenn't Hart man swart is, seggt de Köster, dann hadd hei taun Gräwnis ne rod West antreckt.* —Another one please! *Ja, say das girrl, das money in der cashbox ist nicest, but der cake in der tummy ist nicer!* —*Say der laborer to der farm chief, Tekkin der work easy ist not bein' lazy.* —The boys feel envious on account of all the laughs behind them, so they hurl a few clods of earth back at the girls.

By now the sun has come through. Breakfast. Christa T. straightens up, sees that the field is two thirds clear, and is satisfied. Together with Irene she brings over the coffee and passes it around. The earth on their hands is dry and brittle, which means they must soon get back to work. Then Bodo brings the toad.

It is sitting on his outstretched palm with frightened, bulging eyes. Nobody is surprised when still another bet comes up, but nobody takes Bodo seriously. —What'll you give me if I bite its head off? You? Thirty pfennigs. You? One mark. You? Nothing, it's horrible. Naturally it's nonsense, he's only talking, he won't do it, but all the boys have eager looks on their faces. Irene jumps up and pushes Bodo:

Put it down, the horrible thing! —Bodo replaces the toad among the wet brown leaves.

Then Hammurabi comes up behind him. Why do they call him that and where has he been all this time? —Give it to me! Right, now what do I get if I bite its head off? You? You? You? Some life comes into the proceedings, the answers come more quickly, and the price has gone up, it seems: fifty pfennigs, nothing, you're afraid, one mark, ten pfennigs, if you dare, one mark fifty. —Hammurabi, Christa T. says, too quietly, she feels. Wilhelm! You mustn't do that! She walks up to him, he sidles away. —Five marks eighty, he says. Not much of a deal, but a man's got to live.

Then there's a silence. You can hear the frightened breathing of the toad, you can see the pulsation of its white chest. He won't do it, he won't do it . . . He has bent the front legs down, lunges with his head down to his hand, and bites. Christa T., the teacher, sees his healthy dazzling white teeth bite, once, and again. The toad's head is still firmly attached.

Then the black tomcat smashes against the stable wall, the magpie's eggs splinter against the rock, and again the snow is brushed away from the small rigid face. The teeth bite once more.

It doesn't stop.

Christa T. feels the chill rising up her spine, reaching her head. She turns her head, walks away. It isn't disgust she feels, but sorrow. Later, too, tears run down her face, she crouches by the pathway and weeps. Irene comes and fetches her after a long time has passed. They work in silence until midday.

During the next few days word gets around of her strange behavior, and the biology teacher speaks to her in the corridor: I'm surprised at you, Miss T. I believe you're from the country? And yet you cry about a toad?!

Perusing her notes, I find another scrap of paper which

I'd overlooked before. It's part of the toad manuscript. "Possible conclusion" is the heading. It shows that she couldn't accommodate herself to the true naked reality. She has the village cooking woman come to her before dinner and say: What's happened, miss? That tall, curly-haired boy with the funny name is lying up there in the hay, crying his eyes out. First he came in here with a wild look on his face and cleaned his teeth at the sink like a crazy man, washing his mouth out and all. Then up he goes and lies down in the hay, howling and weeping like a little child.

This conclusion—she must have wanted it badly. And we concur, deeply, with all who desire such conclusions all the more passionately the less often they come to pass. —In reality, the more probable conclusion would have been this: her principal asks her to come to his office. This time she's not offered any coffee. The parents of the student whom people call Hammurabi have put in a complaint about her: for neglecting her duty during the work on the farm. And weren't they right? Not that I want actually to reprimand you, the principal said. You're only a beginner. Didn't you say yourself that this Hamm . . . er, well, this Wilhelm Gerlach worked extremely well? He was one of the best? Good! That's much more important than this silly story about a toad, I think. All the same, it's our responsibility, wouldn't you say? to see that our students don't eat reptiles, at least not while we're present.

He works hard and he's brutish, she told me. It's only his good luck that he's living here. Anywhere else he'd be . . . I don't know what. There's still a demand for people like him. Only don't let's be deceived about that kind of ability. For—what could it lead to?

We didn't know the answer to that question; we knew altogether too little about the way in which time balances things out.

Change of scene—seven years later, disturbing our chronology. Once more she's sitting opposite a student of hers, in the Rila Mountains, sitting in the so-called Monastery Restaurant, having come here with Justus, her husband, on what was to be the last and only journey she made. The young man who approaches them is a medical student, in his last semester at medical school. He introduces himself: Don't you recognize me? He has called Christa T. by her maiden name. —I was the one who always spelled *nämlich* with an *h* in the middle, until you cured me by comparing it with *dämlich*. So I always think of you when I write the word *nämlich*. May I?

He and his fiancée take a seat at the table. The fiancée couldn't be more beautiful and elegant, and she too is to become a doctor. Christa T. shows her amazement, and the student is gratified. He knows the dishes which are brought and says what he thinks of them sensibly, without being dogmatic; he has a sense of humor, he knows his way around, in fact he's not a bad fellow at all. He confesses that if Christa T. had only stayed longer at his school she could have become his favorite teacher. But he adds candidly that her not having stayed also was an advantage for him, because she made such impractical demands. —Just one example: you quoted a phrase to us from a book by some writer or other, I don't recall who it was. It was about the half-real and half-imaginary existence of human beings. It really kept me thinking. —Gorky, says Christa T. So it unsettled you? —Yes, until I began studying, says the medical student. Until I realized that, for me as a doctor, real existence would have to be enough. And God knows we have a fair amount to do with it. When I recognized you just now, your "imaginary existence" came to my mind. Funny, isn't it?

He explains that he has made a discovery and has even managed to put it into words, which is the hardest part of the work; and now he has an insatiable appetite for hearing himself talk about it: the essence of health is adaptation or conformity. He says it again, she needn't raise her eyebrows like that, does she really understand what this means?

Christa T. understood it only too well, she even thought

III

she could happily dispense with his disquisition on biological development, but he's not to be interrupted. To survive, he has realized, has always been man's goal and always will be. This means that at all times conformity is the means of survival: adaptation, conformity at any price.

Hasn't he noticed that he's already used the word at least twice too often?

But you can't upset me now as you used to, I'm not under your moralizing thumb any more, and I'd even go so far as to say this: What could be the result, from a medical standpoint, of a high-minded moral programming of young people, the collision between this morality and the realities of life, which are always stronger, *always,* believe me—now then, what would be the result of such a conflict? Complexes, at best. German educators have always tried to undermine the realities, always ineffectually. The right thing would have been to focus on the realities themselves as the true standard and to measure your success by the degree of psychological robustness you have given your students to sustain them through life. That's what they need most of all, no doubt about it.

Well then, says Christa T., even if she couldn't boast that he's indebted to her for his psychological robustness, she still hopes at least that when he writes his reports for the medical commission he won't ever again write *nämlich* with an *h* in the middle. Sometimes, she adds amiably, one is even satisfied with modest results.

13

Her remark brought more laughter from the medical student.

But that evening Christa T. told her husband Justus that she was really quite glad to have seen him again. Walking in the inner courtyard of the monastery, they come face to face with a fat old monk coming from the kitchen, who pulls something from under his robe and hurriedly swallows it as he walks along. What was that noise? The white cloth is folded and disappears again under the robe. The monk, who is calling the others to worship, enters the courtyard and with a wooden mallet strikes the hollow wooden pipe: ding dong ding. Inside the church, full of wood carvings and golden ornaments, behind the partition which hides the Holy of Holies, a young monk opens the reliquary. The saint's bones behind the sheet of glass. *One after another,* amid interminable chantings, they walk in to kiss the glass, incense candles burn, small gifts are brought. What faces the monks have! Fat thoughtless grizzleheads, lean pale-skinned fanatics, a shifty Burgundian face, an amiable thoughtful scholar, and my dreamer, with the silky hair, who was permitted to open the reliquary.

Let's go to the cloisters, walk beneath the martyrdoms of saints, beneath the Apocalypse which no longer concerns us. One day people will walk like this beneath scenes of our martyrdoms. But the medical student, once a student of mine, is walking around in them today, and none of it is any concern of his—isn't that strange? He showed me in one fell swoop what it really means, this "half-imaginary existence" of human beings—with which, I admit, I was juggling rather in a void in those days. It's our moral existence, that's what it is. And our moral existence is strange enough. Even fantastic. My clever little student didn't think out the consequences; I couldn't teach him to do that. He was a little too happily excited about discovering that he isn't responsible for anything whatever . . .

The tall wooden cross on the western ridge above the valley stands out black against the yellow evening sky. So I suppose, says Christa T., that we can calmly count on our not being bereft of what we still so urgently need.

I don't know if we shall come back again to this journey, her only journey, which she enjoyed so much, because now comes the chapter about Justus. It has been on the way for a long time; her love has already begun, only she knows nothing about it yet.

He first saw her at lunchtime in the commons, when she was still a student. He'd come from another university to attend a conference which still had two more days to run. She's standing in line—who is she, where have I seen her before? That's how it began, at least on one side. He remembers the picture on the wall in his parents' living room, the girl seen in profile, that's who she is, the picture cut from a calendar, portrait of an Egyptian queen.

He asks a mutual friend to take him to her table, and he

invites her to the party at the end of the conference tomorrow evening. She, neither surprised nor offended, simply accepts; no difficulty at all. Except that he cannot, unfortunately, persuade himself that she's particularly interested, likewise the next evening, and the day following the party, when they walk by the canal. Then he has to leave, and he knows: I've made no progress whatever. Although he's never wanted anything more in his life.

Later that must have turned the scales.

It was a long time before we saw him; but we knew from Christa T. herself that someone was in the offing. He's wanted me for a long time.

Then she looked innocently into our inquisitive faces. That was all.

So we'd better take a few steps back.

How young she is! And how she longs to have passionate feelings! Everything she sees is fresh and new, every face, every movement, the whole city, she won't allow anything to be remote or strange, she lives in the present, bewitched by colors, smells, sounds: *Always to be making new connections, always to be moving on from them* . . . The city belongs to her—will she ever be so rich again? The child is hers, sitting forlornly in the corner of a streetcar and asking his mother about everything he can hear outside but not see; the man with black hair—*a lot of white in his narrowed eyes, and a hard trait in his features,* to whom she entrusts tenderness, she feels hot all over when she looks at him, he smiles and says *Auf Wiedersehen* when he leaves. The young gardener from whom she buys the far too expensive lilac and whom she bedazzles: I can't resist such a handsome young man . . . But she gives the lilac to a perplexed husband who comes rushing out of a meeting because he's remembered it's his wedding anniversary and now all the flower shops are closed. And even the lady who comes to visit her son belongs to her, a theology student, Christa T. sizes him up, intelligent but proud: no friend of ours—but then he belongs to her as well.

All this was preparation for her love, for that's what this chapter is about. She sends friendly answers to Justus's letters; then at the right moment his letters stop coming. He had the gift of doing the right thing at the right moment. She liked that. Meanwhile, she didn't lose his telephone number; but it's unlikely she gave it more than a glance or two. One couldn't force her, she couldn't force herself; nothing happened to her quickly, but much had happened already, so now she felt more frequently where it was leading, but this feeling was at once mixed, as was usual for her, with despair: *Suddenly she was seized by a great fear that she couldn't write, wouldn't be able to put into words the feelings that filled her*. In which case it's safer to talk of a third person, whether it's oneself or someone else whom one is calling, for example, "she." One can perhaps slip more easily away from that third person, one doesn't have to be drawn into the *misfortune of her false life,* one can place her side by side with oneself, observe her thoroughly, as one customarily observes other people.

All this could become love, but the decision still has to be taken. One day, when she's once more running across the road, with a crowd of people surging toward her at the intersection, all single people, but every one of them a stranger to her—suddenly she stops, and shudders: Aren't I pretending to myself? How long can one go on waiting? Have I still really got the time? And who precisely does belong to me?

Within an hour she has called the number which, as may be seen, she has been carrying about with her. —So it's you, says Justus, I might have thought it. —That he was tired of waiting, that he was beginning to have doubts and had already been tempted to inquire about her—of all this not a word.

When? he says instead.

That's the right beginning for something that's going to last.

But I can't promise, she tells herself, as she walks from the telephone booth, of course I can't promise anything.

While writing this—in all good conscience, because every statement is doubly authenticated and stands up to the scrutiny of review—while leafing further through the reddish-brown Berlin notebook and coming upon the line "Justus, dear beloved Justus!", while endeavoring to create the room in which their first meeting can occur—while all this is going on an old mistrustfulness overcomes me again, though I thought I had quelled it, I wouldn't have expected it to return at this of all moments. Mightn't the net that has been woven and set for her finally turn out to be incapable of catching her? The sentences I have written, yes. Also the ways she has traveled, a room she has lived in, a landscape near and dear to her, a house, even a feeling—but not herself. For she's hard to catch. Even if I could do it, faithfully present everything about her that I've known or experienced, even then it's conceivable that the person to whom I tell the story, whom I need and whose support I solicit, might finally know nothing about her.

As good as nothing.

Unless I can contrive to say the most important thing about her, which is this: Christa T. had a vision of herself. I can't prove this in the way that I could prove she lived here or there, at this time or that, and that she read this book or that from the university library. But the books are neither here nor there, I haven't looked up her old library cards; if the worst came to the worst, I'd simply invent a few titles. No, one doesn't invent a person's visions, though one does sometimes find them. I've known of her vision for a long time: since that moment twelve years before, when I saw her blowing a trumpet.

For we're now in the year 1955.

It's a long time before we see Justus, as I've said; he was withheld from us. And besides, we were wondering: a vet's wife in Mecklenburg, was that to be it? For one is always involuntarily grasping for definitions. But then came the fancy-dress ball, at which Christa T. arrived as Sophie La Roche, though she hadn't dressed up at all, she wore only her goldish-brown dress with the exotic pattern, telling everyone who she was supposed to be. Justus beside her, no more dressed up than she herself, was playing the part of Lord Seymour, at least that's what he said. Nobody knew whether this idea was exceptionally lofty or simply contrary; but in any case we could at last take a look at Justus, and in doing so we found that we could quietly drop all the definitions.

It was, I suppose, what people call a party, one of the first, and we weren't at all sure how things are done at parties. Yet when we looked at our hosts we felt that a party was what it had to be: as people arrived they were told to do as they pleased, *vorurteilsfrei*—don't be afraid! and Christa T. nodded sensibly, looked around in the two dimly lit rooms, plucked a few paper streamers from the rubber plant and draped them around her shoulders, emptied a package of confetti over Justus's head, and said: This place is all right.

I can't say I shared her feeling. I felt she'd planned something special for this evening and it couldn't be properly accommodated in this society where all the costumes looked provocative and yet so repressed. Her plan seemed to be aimed against Justus himself, or at him. I didn't know what to do. I even wanted to warn him, side with him, I liked him. Then I saw that he didn't need any warnings. He kept quite cool, for his time of uncertainty had passed long ago.

And hers? Or was it she who was mutely asking for some kind of support? —Mademoiselle La Roche, I said, when nobody could hear us, you don't seem to realize what you're taking upon yourself: the fate of La Roche! An over-ardent and rather sentimental dreamer, chained to a life in the country against her will, so that she pours all her ungratified longing into an invented character . . .

Much worse than that, Christa T. replied. If it was La Roche, things wouldn't be so bad. But it's that character who's meant, Fräulein von Sternheim herself: and her fate.

You're joking, I said.

Justus brought some champagne and stood there beside us. But I could go on talking.

Seduction? Intrigues? A false marriage with this rogue Derby? A mournful country life in the English provinces? And, for God's sake, virtue?!

Precisely that, said Christa T. And finally her reward for everything: Lord Seymour, the paragon!

Mademoiselle, said Justus, you shouldn't call me that.

We'll see what you'll be called, Christa T. said.

She drank off her champagne in one gulp, looking at him. His smile was hopeful, but not self-confident.

It was working out, it really could work out.

I thought I could now see her plan more clearly. She had found a way to show him what she'd be giving up if she went along with him. She seemed to have just realized this herself, and she was scared again, it was a crucial moment. But Justus, whether he knew it or not, did the right thing: he behaved as if he'd known this long before she did, as if this was precisely the vital point, as if there was no question of giving anything up. And he was telling her so, without wasting a word, simply by the way he raised his glass to her, took her glass from her hand, and led her away to dance. Since, as he saw, her decision had been made, it was up to him to make the last step easy for her: there was to be no last step, only one step among many others.

She was grateful to him for the certainty he gave her, and with good reason. Then he let her dance for as long as she liked and with whomever she liked, didn't dance himself, didn't drink much, waited until he could say: Let's go. — Then she left her partner standing and went at once. She waved to me airily and left us, and those of us who stayed behind might well ask ourselves why we'd ever doubted that she'd get married in a simple happy way.

That evening she wanted to take herself and us a few steps back, one or two centuries back, so as to see ourselves more clearly. In a hundred years, no, in fifty, we too shall be historical figures standing on a stage. Why wait so long? Why, since after all it's inevitable, why not take a few strides and jump on the stage oneself, try out a few of the roles, before one defines oneself, rejecting this one or that as too tall an order, finding others already occupied and feeling secretly envious of their occupants: but finally to accept one role in which everything depends on how you play it, depends thus on you and you alone. Hers: the wife of a man who'll be a veterinary surgeon and who knows that she not only sought him out but created him especially, and that each must compel the other to live to the full extent of their powers, if they are never to lose one another again.

That evening he took her home with him. I've given up the idea of inventing the room, it's not important. And now she doesn't need time any more. The playing was over, the role lapsed into irrelevancy, he loved her.

14

Now one must be twice as cautious. It's hard to avoid the insistent feeling that one has found the key.

It's a question of allaying one's suspicions. Is this the key—a few scattered words: "imaginary existence," "vision" . . . And what if there were many doors? And what if this door had only been hit upon by chance, through guess-work?

Would other doors never have opened, even for Christa T.?

We can make another attempt: it wasn't the fancy-dress ball, which was an invention in any case, but a simple arrival, an arrival, what's more, in a small country town. There's no point in giving its name, they're all alike, except that in this one Justus happens to be working as an assistant. And so Christa T. will visit him, on a Sunday, traveling by the afternoon train. Sorry, I can't make it earlier. I mightn't go there at all, easy enough, she tells herself; but now she's already on the train—what does that prove? That's how Justus talks, he's a Pomeranian, from a family of farmers, that's the way they are; she can't help smiling. It doesn't mean anything, and it mustn't.

The weather couldn't be better. A family boards the train —young man, grim-looking wife, and a boy, with all their luggage, equipped for a long journey. The man collapses on a heavy rucksack and falls asleep. The woman sits across and scowls at him all the time demandingly, small drops of sweat on her face. She bends forward as if not to lose sight of him. She has a healthy, heavy body, a fleshy head, dark-blond hair combed back, but she can't rely just on herself, she has to screw into her earlobes these silvery shining pendants, a sharp contrast to her darkly passionate look.

If she was thinking that her old habit of observing people would distract her . . . Will he be waiting there or not? How will he look at me, what will be the first thing he says?—all this will be decisive. It's certain he'll be there, however. And his look goes right through me in any case, even if I'm only picturing him, as I've been doing so often this past week, and it's not getting any less keen . . . And nothing he could say would tip the scales against him now.

But I can do as I please, can't I?

The young man has finally woken up, his first look meets his wife's, then she looks away, tugs at her son, he has to make room for his father. All movements end in some result or other, you aren't young and green any more, twenty-six now, and you've been feeling one can be too indecisive, that indecision—or what should one call it?—can make you miss the right moment for love, for life, for everything for which there's no substitute. So must you accept certain ties?

Justus was looking in her direction, his look was just as she wished it to be, he noticed everything: how long she'd stood before the mirror, that her hair was short; but all she felt was that her reservations were melting away as she walked toward him, and when she was close enough to him she'd lost all memory of her doubts. Thus it was, and thus it remained.

Naturally she was also looking for protection; perhaps that should have been said earlier; and who'd think any the worse of her for it? To build dikes against excessive demands, fantastic wishes, erratic dreams. To take in one's hand a thread which continues always and through all circumstances, to which one can hold tight, when necessary; the old thread, made of small skills of the hand and of simple activities. Skills and activities which one can maintain or relinquish because they keep life itself going. To bring children into the world, to take upon oneself all the troubles to which they owe their lives. To prepare a thousand meals, always to see that the washing is done. To do your hair the way your husband likes it; smile when he needs it; be ready for love.

She sees the advantage of being a woman.

At that time she must have changed.

Putting it bluntly, one would have to say that she was beautiful and strange and happy, as she looks in the photographs of our New Year's festivities. Beautiful and strange because she was happy—I see now that unhappiness makes people alike, but happiness doesn't, it makes them individuals. From the photographs one can see how she could laugh, even that she could still be astonished by colored candles. What one doesn't see is that she was taking herself seriously. She was remaking herself from the roots, for Justus, which Lord knows was no trouble but the greatest earthly pleasure that had ever come her way. The most banal things—and she could draw the pleasure out of them at least, and sometimes real joy, it was incredible. The village policeman, she said, who hauled Justus over the coals because he was sneaking to the pond with the goldfish bowl under his arm: do you know what he wanted to do? Simply put the goldfish back in. Very shady dealings there. Ah, you can't see it, the abashed look on his face, but I can.

She could visualize anyone anywhere, as long as she had a

I

few solid ingredients, like a goldfish and a village police-man. She even stuck a beard on her chin to help us see how he looked, but it fell off when we clinked glasses for the New Year. Nineteen fifty-six. Now we need every single year, magnanimity is a bygone; perhaps we'll have to learn to count in days. And in hours.

By then she was a married woman, it happened very quickly, the child was already on the way: Klein-Anna, she called her. But before this the pains had begun, facial pains, nervous pains, a family complaint, sometimes hard to bear. She was almost astonished, as if she'd been expecting all adversities to stop of their own accord, now that she'd begun to understand how to take and give her part of the world's work, for so it was. Nothing, nothing pointed to the fact that she'd simply be cut down in her thirty-fifth year; everything seemed set to continue slowly and steadily, exist-ence to the end. But since there is no end, only this meaning-less misfortune, one must try to extend the lines of this life she left, with due caution, and in its natural perspective. So that people may see her.

How well I can see her—no matter what she's doing. Roasting a saddle of pork, perhaps, crisp and scored when it comes from the oven; it gives her pleasure. Or she takes care of the children, feeds them, teaches them things; or she's making tea for Justus, in the complicated way he likes. I was there when she was looking at curtain material for her house; the curtains are still there, but she isn't. —I mustn't go on like this. I'm anticipating, as if her everyday skills could prove or even cancel anything. As if there were some court to which one can appeal on such grounds as these—her being useful, her having been put to use—which might at least feel something.

But for another six motley months before marrying she lives in Berlin. The reddish-brown notebook simply goes si-lent; its last pages are filled with recipes and household ac-counts; it makes me laugh, her allocation of this or that tiny sum of money. She closes the book and says, We're off. Sometimes they travel far, sometimes *"drüben"*—over there. The trip there is unusual enough to make your heart beat faster: over there is where the opposite ideas for living are produced, where everything is the reverse—people, things, and thoughts; that's the real reason why you feel uneasy when you turn the next corner, full of weird expectation, to find always only the same smiling traffic policeman. But one might just as easily catch oneself napping: this is a twofold country and, what's more, everyone in it is twofold, one part possibility and the other its refutal. One gets rid of the feeling of confusion at times by doing something violent. She spits on the memorial to "the stolen territories in the East." Memory's color is greenish-gold, it mustn't go black, mustn't go dry: black is the color of guilt. She spits on this black stone.

Come on, Justus says, his hand circling her upper arm. They walk up a carpeted staircase; Christa T. at every turn twiddles the brass knobs on the handrail. She'd like best to count the steps, to avoid the sight of the door plates which are approaching her now, but here they are, there's Justus's family name again, here's his cousin's elegant apartment, they've come to visit his relatives. Nice people, but you'll see for yourself. She's a little bit like you, but don't worry. She's my favorite cousin, she'll be very nice to you.

He shouldn't have said that.

Now she starts by looking for the similarity, which keeps her from joining in the conversation; his beautiful cousin will think I'm silly; we certainly don't have long eyelashes like hers. Perhaps they're false. Dearest, they say. But that's surely what people call one another in novels, we ought just to use the familiar "du," then we shan't feel strange, but I don't mind. I'll get around it by not calling her anything.

Then she gets a shock when she hears they're both—almost—the same age; she blurts out—It can't be!—bites her lip and blushes. The cousin smiles.

Justus is standing beside the cousin's husband, who's explaining what his work at the stock exchange really involves. Could you start all over again, please, slowly, as for a beginner. I never could understand a thing about it, because I don't see what is at the back of all the machinery—you might as well be talking Chinese.

That's Justus all over, says the cousin, very content. It's all the same for him to ask the same question a hundred times over—he's just acting simple. But Justus is now in full swing, trying to prove to Siegfried he's superfluous because his work isn't productive. God, that's not Siegfried's weak point. They stare at one another for a moment. But I know Justus, and I know a bit about his way of thinking; I studied economics once for a few semesters in East Berlin. Every system has its logic, once you've accepted its premises, don't you find? So one slips into the system, really, I know what I'm talking about. Suddenly you start jabbering about "meaning" and "responsibility" yourself, all these grand words . . .

Luckily she found herself talking, just in time, about the frailty of human nature. You needn't look at me so severely! says the cousin. But Christa T. wasn't looking severe, she'd only been thinking that the idea of human frailty suited the cousin well, and that the cousin knew it and it was only because of this that she'd brought it up—there really aren't many ideas to choose from. But she's got nothing at all against people who go on believing in human goodness, or whatever you want to call it, after they've passed twenty-five, really she hasn't. Idealism—everybody longs for it sometimes, don't they? We on this side, you know, are really terribly materialistic; and you're very sensitive about that, you can smell it out, you wrinkle your nose the moment you come into the place.

Did I wrinkle my nose? asks Christa T. in astonishment.

The cousin laughs, as she used to laugh long ago, and Justus looks across and Christa T. knows why she's his favorite cousin. Then she admits that she did wrinkle her nose, except she doesn't say why she did so, but it's enough to call for a whisky to celebrate this new understanding between them, Scotch, on the rocks. But surely it can't be your first ever? God, what a lot life's got in store for you. And to think of all the waters I've been washed in . . .

Waters! says Siegfried. You're underrating yourself. And he reels off a few brands of liquor, amazing how many he knows.

Then a few aunts come in, with a wave of sympathy, and terrible words tumble from their candid lips. Terror, they say, eating nutcake, you poor souls, they treat you so you don't even miss It . . . Miss who did you say? the cousin asks. Aunt Hermine's face fills with reproof: Not who, my dear, she says; and from her mouth comes, mysteriously, the watchword: Freedom!

The cousin takes Christa T. into the kitchen. You can't choose your relatives, she says; and she begins to pack bottles of spices into a small folding bag. Take these with you, you can't get them, I know, and Justus loves spicy food, yes, I insist, I know Justus. Or shall I give you a bra? Here's the tea that he likes best, he'll show you how to make it; I told him how. Don't worry, he's yours now. But you'll come and see us sometimes, won't you? Tell me whatever you need; don't be embarrassed or I'll be cross. Why shouldn't Siegfried's immoral money help you to beautify your moral lives . . . And when your baby comes, I'll see that you get some bananas.

But how did you know that I . . .

The cousin can't manage anything better than a look of sympathy. What a couple of characters you are, she says.

Justus thought she'd held her own very well; but now, he said, we must get married. No onlookers, please, no announcements for anyone, the lady official at the courthouse gets nervous, feels she's only being tolerated, so she makes it short. They both say yes; then they splurge on a taxi, which takes them to the new restaurant in the Stalinallee, and there they order a mixed grill and ice cream. I wasn't there, but at some point during the day Christa T. must have reminded her husband that every good love story comes to an end in marriage. Probably by then they were in their big empty room, with nothing but a wide mattress in it; and the moment arrived when they realized that real ecstasy doesn't last for the day when one expects it. They felt fine enough, she says, when they were at the opera in the evening; but at intermission she had to leave, she wasn't feeling well. He can't get her to talk about it. You're just an animal doctor, she says; he gets furious at his helplessness; and that was their wedding night. The next day she has to go into the hospital, an old complaint has returned; the doctor says it's due to the baby, but the baby could also cure it. A child prodigy, she says to Justus, who has to go back to his practice.

Will you write?

But she can't write because she can't bear to think of him so intensely; she wrote things in her little brown notebook; probably to this day he doesn't know why he never received letters from her. When I saw her again she was lying in a hospital bed, feeling half guilty and half annoyed, but in any case married and about to have a child. She was reading *The Magic Mountain* and making efforts to sink into the same kind of vague time-flux: otherwise I couldn't stand it, she says.

I didn't ask what she couldn't stand. They were seldom apart during their seven years of marriage; Justus gave me, with her other papers, two or three letters to him which she never mailed. They belong to a later period. He'd never read them, and he gave them to me, as if I were entitled to read them first . . . But perhaps now I really am entitled to do so. I read them and found that she'd become more level-headed. Then I read them again and was amazed at my blindness, for suddenly I noticed how shy she was in these old letters, as one notices in a certain light the colors reappearing in an old picture. I'd like to ask Justus if he knew she was shy of him. But he won't know, and I won't ask; I won't even wonder where the shyness came from, as well as the undertone of wooing in her letters; for only a person who gets his feelings from trashy literature could expect any feeling, especially such a composite one as the feeling called "love," to remain constant; and such constancy is certainly not desirable. As the years passed, she must gradually have forgotten how to keep an eye on herself; that, at least, is how the letters sound. In the end—I mean the actual end—there's never a sign of her refusing to write in order to lessen her sufferings when someone is expecting news of her. She continues to write letters from the hospital, including those two which she sent to her children.

Promises she knows she won't keep.

15

Now that I'm noticing things about her which other people
—perhaps—have overlooked, I must naturally ask if there
weren't things about her which I never saw and never shall
be able to see because my focus was wrong. Seeing has little
to do with the heart's resolutions. So I shall visit her in the
hospital again, that Sunday in autumn, after her wedding
day, in search of what I've overlooked. I have a reason for
repeating the visit: it's because I was never with her when
she was really sick. That sounds like self-reproach, and it is;
but I had good reasons for not doing so, just as everyone
has good reasons. My best reason was that I couldn't believe
that she was being serious.

It was a day like today in September, both hot and mild. I
took off my jacket and carried it over my arm as I walked
from the Friedrichstrasse station up the Luisenstrasse,
which seemed endless. Only when I reached the entrance to

the clinic, after I'd already lost my way, did it occur to me to look at the sky. It was slightly hazed over, as it is today; and today again I feel what I felt then in a wordless way: a sharp pain, because this pale familiar blue, which seemed to be made only for us, and to belong only to us, is to be found in old pictures, where nothing but this blue strikes a chord in my feelings. I felt indignant that a hundred years from now, long after we've disappeared, this impartial and unchanged blue will still materialize because of a certain season of the year, a certain whim of the light.

This thought hurt me, and suddenly the ugly red of the clinic walls hurt me too, and the naked echo of my footsteps on the worn stairs. I felt sure that it would hurt me even to see her. There she lay in the last bed of a long row; and on the opposite side of the ward there were just as many beds, at least twenty. It was no place for a long-delayed reunion: when I saw her lying there it did seem she'd been away a long time and as if she must have changed a lot.

Eventually she put on her robe and came out with me into the corridor. We stood by the window, I remember, and talked about the woman in the bed next to Christa T.'s, a streetcar conductress.

They don't understand what happens to them, said Christa T.; and I wanted her to be less tolerant about it, even if she couldn't break down the young woman's resignation, her weary surrender to the sufferings inflicted on her by her husband. For us there was no question: it was up to Christa T. to try to do this; for we felt bound by a promise, which we had never really given, but the promise was more binding than any real vow: to help everyone, no matter whom. Then you see this woman lying there, and she can't be helped, and you feel you've broken your word.

They don't even *know* that they don't understand anything, Christa T. added, and when she reads a newspaper she wouldn't dream of thinking it's herself the newspaper is talking about.

Teach her, I said. It seemed to us a sort of test, whether

this streetcar conductress could be roused to assert her rights, her own proper rights.

He beats her, Christa T. said, he rapes her, and now she's had her third abortion.

Report him to the police, I said.

No matter what I suggest, she rejects it, and she's told me so. If I so much as touch on the subject now, she won't speak another word to me.

We began to argue. In the end I had to realize that nothing could be done without the woman's consent. That she would stay bogged down in the life she had brought into the world with her; and that there were people like herself to whom all her impatience was of no help or use whatever. We both felt bitter about it, it was as if we were reproaching one another. Today I know that this kind of embitteredness doesn't disappear, and that we'd always share it. At that time it seemed to divide us; we misunderstood one another.

We were standing by the window, at the end of the long hospital corridor, we'd said all we had to say and were looking out of the window in silence. Then a sudden gust of wind came and a great flock of crows crossed the sky, all of them, so it seemed to us, suddenly uttering a cry. Just this very moment the same flock of crows has crossed the same sky; and now that whole afternoon comes back to me: the drab hospital corridor, the narrow window, our argument, our common bitterness. And the certainty that she was still capable of being bitter.

That's my reason for talking about it: bitterness as the fruit of passion. Is that phrase old? Will it seem surprising? Funny? Old-fashioned? Will anyone consider relating it to a hospital corridor, lecture rooms, to work parties moving over the wreckage of cities, violent discussions, conversations, speeches, books? Or will people keep trying to make us believe that passion has everlastingly had to do with the officer with a mania for honor who dies in a duel, or with the rise and fall of monarchs and leaders?

It gives one a good feeling to be at the beginning of

things. One loves that feeling, and one's only anxiety comes with the fear that one might fail to live up to the passion at large in society. Like ourselves, Christa T. had the luck to be forced to create her identity at an age when one is passionate. With that as the standard, all other attractions are shallow; and if anyone—Justus's cousin, for instance—argues that people can be bought, all Christa T. can do is raise her eyebrows, which makes her look arrogant.

Then came a night that was unusually dark. We happened to be together and from all the Western radio stations, among the reports of fighting in Budapest, we heard the loud and almost blatant laughter at the demise of what they called Utopia.

Now Justus's cousin is thinking they were right, Christa T. said.

We didn't know what that night meant; it has taken us years to find out. Except that the struggles of the older generation suddenly became our own struggles; we felt this at once, and very distinctly. And that they wouldn't allow us to retreat into the roles of dupes. But the role of the iron believer was now defunct as well; the stage on which such roles had been played was plunged in darkness. Yes, there had been a sudden change in the lighting and we hadn't foreseen it. Only later did we ask ourselves: And why not? That night, over our tea, which got cold, while the sneering voices gathered in our room, we noticed only the darkening of the world, and didn't notice that what had been extinguished was only the spotlights, and that we'd have to get used now to seeing by the sober light of real days and nights.

A word came up, as if newly invented: truth. We kept repeating it, truth, truth, and believed the word was more closely than ever our concern, truth, as if it were some animal with small eyes which lives in the dark and is timid but which one can surprise and catch, to possess it for all time. Just as we'd possessed our earlier truths. Then we checked ourselves. Nothing is so difficult as turning one's attention to things as they really are, to events as they really occur, after one has spent a long time not doing so and has mistaken their reflection in wishes, beliefs, and judgments for the things and events themselves. Christa T. realized that we all had to accept a share in the mistakes we'd made, otherwise we'd have no share in the truths. She always looked people straight in the eye; so she wasn't downcast by certain kinds of looks now. She was more shaken by the sight of tears in eyes that had never wept before.

Her first child was born during this time, and the delivery was difficult. The child was in a bad position. For hours she strained uselessly. Of course it weakened her, but she didn't retreat into the feeling that the pains were an injustice being done to her. She had no sentimentality to spare and couldn't forget that she wanted to have the child and that the strict rhythm of rending strain and relaxation was necessary to produce it. Later too she never said that she'd had enough and couldn't be expected to have any more children. She only cried when the doctor brought the child to her and when she called it by name: Anna. What are you up to, Anna, you've made a good start, I must say. She'd expected to be happy, or at least to feel something she'd felt before; but this was an unknown feeling, and she went overboard. Well, well, she said inaudibly to the baby, and to herself, it was like it and not like it, but all's well, let's be quiet now, it's not so very extraordinary.

Does one remember tenderness? Is it tenderness the child still knows today when it hears the words "your mother"? Even if the child has outgrown the tenderness it might be able to remember? Or can the child remember nothing at all, not even that?

The child will be shown the small house in the small Brandenburg town. That's where you were living. This is where you learned to walk; you crept through the hole in the fence, went to the edge of the forest, it wasn't far, and you fell asleep in a hollow among the heather and small pine trees; your mother was half dead with anxiety . . .

Then the child will think it remembers what it can't remember; and the lush images it is shown will forever suppress the shadows that sometimes appear behind its closed eyelids and which are more true than the plumped-out images. The child, Anna, will look at the lake and believe that this is the lake of her earliest years. But how could it be? In those days it wasn't a lake, it was water, absolutely water; and the hundred and fifty yards to the shore, that was the way to it, long and broad, who knows, it might become to her the original of all ways. The day comes when she understands her shadow, tries it out by making movements, grasps it. To forget. To forget the earliest fears: darkness, when one comes into the loggia at nightfall, the stray dog which Father drove away with loud cursing, so that the next day and the day after it you stood where he stood, cursing loudly, looking fierce, but there's no dog. The magic worked. Worst of all, the fly circling the lamp every morning when you wake. Your mother can chase it away. To forget.

Christa T. had forgotten nothing. Presumably she found that one is well off if one performs all the little services the child needs, without asking how one knows them and why one is utterly at peace when one leans over the bed and breathes the warm fragrance that comes from a sleeping child. It was a good year, a year of transition, the little house wasn't their own but they were happy in it; they were carried along with it in a current which favored them, with the little house and the child, they were like a small family which didn't know when and where they would reach land and finally start being serious about things.

Justus says to me: If only we hadn't lived later as if we might have to leave at any moment. Because we certainly didn't mean to stay there. I think we both agreed on this from the first moment, although we only talked about it later. So we didn't even arrange a regular bedroom. You've seen her bed, this couch behind the cupboard, how bitter she must have felt waking up there sometimes.

I don't know what he really thought about it; but I think she'd have felt even worse waking up in a regular bedroom, every morning looking at a cupboard that stands immovably in its place, while for her the ordinary adult life, the life of people who have regularized themselves, had still not yet begun. She was always, to her own way of thinking, a person with prospects, latent possibilities.

You haven't understood a thing if you shrug your shoulders, turn away, turn from her, Christa T., and attend to grander and more useful lives. My concern is to attend to her. To the richness she revealed, to the greatness she could attain, to the usefulness at her command. Thus also to this Mecklenburg town, rising up out of the fields of potatoes and rye, a picture-book town, with a row of red barns, a humpbacked cobble street leading to the marketplace, church, pharmacy, store, café. As she approaches it and sees that it is just so, Christa T. can't help laughing: but it's not the laugh of a conqueror. The outcome isn't so certain. But she laughs because the town is still a town, doesn't melt when you take a good look at it, doesn't tip over when you touch it. And yet what else did she think? That it could never be serious? That seriousness couldn't be made of stone and cement? A corner house, for example, a row of windows on the upper floor, with a view over two country roads that intersect in front of the house, a yard with a large chestnut tree, the worn cold stone staircase, the ugly brown door, with a name plate on it . . . She's about to move on, with a sigh of relief; but it's her own name. So in she goes.

Be quiet now, Anna.

She carries the child along the long corridor into a room; there's a bed in it, she puts the child on the bed. Quiet now.

She walks through the other rooms, all of them large and bare, she walks to the windows, sees lime trees, half-timbered houses. So this is it. It resists her. As she turns, Justus appears in the door. She gives herself a shake. Might as well be here as anywhere, she says.

But they're not so unimportant, the places we live in.

They aren't only the framework for our actions, they involve themselves in the actions, they change the scenery; and not infrequently, when we say "circumstances," what we really mean is a particular place which never became interested in us.

Christa T. couldn't say that she hadn't chosen her own role, and she didn't say it. On the contrary, she titled herself, with irony of course, in one of her infrequent letters, "veterinary surgeon's wife in a small Mecklenburg town"; and she added, as if to mitigate her amazement, a word or two of doubt: Shall I ever learn? Every horse that dies, every cow that calves, is a catastrophe for me.

The real gist of what she meant is contained in her statement: "No more playing with possible variants." It was a cryptic statement, but today its meaning is clear. No more moving at will from role to role, from stage to stage, or simply hiding behind the curtain. Then came the sequence of eight words announcing the title which she had to accept.

Now she would have to answer the question: what are you going to be? She would have to say: I mean to get up early every morning, first to look after the child and then see to breakfast for Justus and me; while I'm doing things I shall listen to the instructions for the day; I shall note that I must call up the district vet and where I can reach Justus if farmer Ulrich of Gross-Bandikow telephones about his pigs. I shall stand in the doorway holding the coffee pot, and I shall of course understand expressions like "cattle brucellosis" and "calving" and "tuberculin-tested"; and every morning I shall be for a moment surprised to have just heard these words that I shall go on hearing for twenty years without surprise. Yes, I shall say, the hypodermics are sterilized, and the girl assistant for the pig inoculations is coming the day after tomorrow. Don't worry, I won't be far from the telephone. Are you really worried about Ulrich's pigs?

Then I shall go down to the yard. I shall get into the car while Justus is warming up the engine, while it's gradually getting lighter outside, though in here it's still dark, and we're alone. Justus is beginning to look attentive. I like him best when he has that look, so I'll quietly say: Stay a minute! and he'll smile and stay a minute. Then I'll watch him drive away, walk slowly up the stairs and do all day the things that have to be done, one thing after another, so that my work propels the day along; that's how it often seems.

But the day is so heavy my two hands won't in the long run have the strength.

16

I ask Justus: So was she afraid she wouldn't be strong enough?

Justus says: Yes; and after a pause: No.

He doesn't say anything more, and it's difficult to explain how in some ways Christa T. always felt inadequate, in others able to manage, perhaps even superior. Sometimes I think she misled us all and herself as well, with her laments about her inadequacy. For example, the delicate balance that she knew how to maintain in her housekeeping seems to me to have been too complicated to have been a matter of chance. Here one weak point would be checked by another, out of two omissions could arise an astounding improvisation, one always had the notion that one shouldn't touch anything or else the whole edifice would come tumbling down, whereas she herself, if it came to that, would take a firm grasp with both hands—all of this one might have called sophisticated if it hadn't been for her tiredness, which told another story. In the last years . . . There, I've said it, and I won't withdraw it as I've done before now—because these *are* the last years: in the last years we never saw her otherwise than tired. Today one can ask, to be sure, what this tiredness meant, but at that time the question wasn't asked because it would have been meaningless. The answer would have helped neither her nor us. This much is certain: what one does can never make one so tired as what one doesn't do or cannot do. That was the case with her. That was her weakness and her secret superiority.

Had she changed? I asked Justus.

You mean . . . Yes, he said. You wouldn't have recognized her.

And—she knew . . .

I don't know, he said. We had stopped talking about it. But it was noticeable that she didn't ask about the children any more. Not a word. Can you imagine that?

I've seen the two letters, they're on the table beside me. Blue envelopes with cellophane windows, her last letters to her two older children, neither of whom could read. She cut blue fishes and yellow flowers out of colored paper and pasted them like an ornamental frame around the margins of the white paper; she painted big clear letters, wrote about the springtime and summer, for it was in the depth of winter when she was taken sick, frost and ice when she died. How I'd love to go skating with you now on the lake! She writes about sowing radishes and planting flowers, and about learning to swim in the lake. The envelopes, into which I put back the letters, are already yellow and brittle at the edges. I shall give back the letters; perhaps the children want to read them now.

She didn't ask about them any more? I ask Justus.

Not a word, he says. Two or three weeks, not a word, and then the end.

Do you think, I say, that she didn't say anything because it might have weakened her?

But she was already weak. She wanted me not to see it.

That's what I'd call strength.

So I push her along before me, her weakness, her strength, and this is how we gradually get used to her death. A dike built against time, and time seems hostile to me, but she is indifferent. She doesn't need to do anything, the time is coming up to the limit set for her, for Christa T.: then her time is up, and only our time is left.

Let's forget what we know, otherwise we shall see her only obscurely. We can enter the years that she entered: into a time that is great and infinite. Not as into a trap with the trigger set, shifting a millimeter every day till the trap is shut. But as if we were entering life.

We already know about her wonder at being where she was. In the last years it increases, becoming almost disbelief. It was beyond all imagining—for she's no dreamer—that everything should be as one has imagined it. That nothing remarkable should happen in between seemed to her remarkable beyond belief. And her feelings told her how dangerous it can be to be safe. The harmlessness of the dentist's wife, whom, coffee cup in hand, she must have been staring at for a long time. Now the dentist's wife stands, says goodbye, walks out with a rather stiff back; or does she? From the square outside she looks back and up to the window where Christa T. is standing, smiling in a way that isn't allowed here. The dentist's wife and the school principal's wife won't be able to explain to their husbands why the vet's wife isn't quite the right company for them; one can't blame them for not being able to describe a smile. It must suffice to mention that the dentist's wife spent more than a day reconstructing her tidy life to fortify it against this smile, telling herself she's a respectable housewife and spouse and occupies her position in the moral order of the world—and not the lowest position either. She doesn't say anything malicious about Christa T.; altogether she's an amiable woman, unable, also, to find the precise expression for her feelings. Otherwise she'd have probably called

Christa T. "not a very serious young woman." When she thinks of a particular look that Christa T. can give, she even murmurs to herself: "Weird, that's what it is."

For to many people wonderment is weird. One shouldn't, especially when visitors are present, look around one's own living room as if it had suddenly become a foreign place, as if the tables and chairs could suddenly walk away on their own feet and the walls suddenly sprout holes.

Nevertheless, the dentist's wife and the principal's wife can simply stay away, can speak ill or be amiable and silent. We cannot stay away when things get difficult, and we must speak of her. There are several possible approaches here, even if the framework is firm and cannot be expanded much. The first testimonies would be the occasional letters we exchanged. Second, the scraps of paper with jottings about her children. For when Anna was three, Lena was born, in all respects the opposite of her sister: dark and delicate and sensitive. If I've complained about the disorder and volatility of her papers up till now—what am I to say about this bundle of papers. It's as if she never had a notebook within reach these days, not even a writing pad, but only envelopes, the backs of bills, memoranda—cast-off scraps from her husband's desk.

The third possible approach to these years would simply be memory. It seems easy to picture Christa T. walking up the stairs, a bundle wrapped in blankets on her arm—Anna —and her calling out to us from the stairs that she's terribly tired, and then our sitting there together, half the night, even if it's only because we think we're making the most of the time. —This would be the picture I see.

Everything points to transience. Nothing stays as it is. The signs we make are provisional; if one knows it, well and good. Her letters, hurried and sporadic, out of date, by-gone things, and the tone of abjection that creeps into them, never really taken seriously. These notes—nothing but promises made to herself, echoes of a habit she can't break.

Our short encounters—a start only, while we waited for the times when we'd really meet.

Images lose now their firm outlines. We're approaching the vague territory of the present. Perhaps one can hear what one doesn't see.

I hear her saying: We don't see one another often enough.

I hear her tormenting herself. The proof of the person she was would lie in these words: We don't see one another often enough. She craves meaning, significance.

But does it matter?

She insists that it does. We must know what has happened to us, she said. One must know what happens to oneself.

But why? What if it would paralyze us?

Her idea was that doing things blind or deaf means only being blind and deaf to things. She was for clarity and consciousness; but she didn't think, as many people do, that it takes no more than a little courage, no more than the surfaces of events which are easily called truth, no more than a little chatter about "getting on fine, thank you."

Peace was suddenly an important word; reason, we thought, reason and science, the scientific age. Then at night we went out on the balcony to watch for a few moments the faint trace of new stars moving along the horizon. The discovery that the world, released from iron definitions, was coming back within our reach, that it seemed to need us, with all our imperfections, imperfections one can admit, now that they don't mean one might be dragged by them into the abyss . . .

She believed that you must work at your past as you work at your future; I find this in notes she made on books she'd read. A publisher had asked her to write something about this; but because of her increasing tiredness and sickness she never got further than making these notes; and I'm sure that she would have kept to the criteria which she sets in them, without fluttering an eyelid. Not that she'd have expected perfection, but she wants everything to be new and fresh, nothing should be colorless and fortuitous and banal as in reality, something else should be there, not always the same old events and worldwide announcements. Original-ity, she notes, and then: jettisoned, because of cowardice. She wrote: Perhaps in life one can make certain cuts; but not here.

The happy times of pristine thinking and open minds, always favorable for beginnings, belonged now to the past, and we knew it. We tipped the last of the wine into the apple tree. The new star hadn't appeared. We were cold and went back into the room, where the moonlight was coming in. Her child was asleep, she went to the bedside and looked at the child for a long time. One can't have everything, everyone knows that, but what's the use of knowing?

Perhaps in life one can make certain cuts? . . . But when she was alone, she stood at the front door, looked down the long hallway, felt the silence beginning to clutch her, and she said aloud: No.

As often as possible she drove about in the countryside with her husband. Her old greed for faces, the way they really look, receiving bad news or good, tensing, resolving, doubting, wavering, understanding, overcoming. She for-gets herself when she sees the wild peasant faces. Justus has to go into their houses. What does the Herr Doktor hon-estly think about the cooperatives? Justus brings statistical charts: production of milk, pork, cereals. The world record, compared with their own region. Christa T. saw that so much had never been asked of them before, an unprece-dented step beyond their apparent maximum capacity. She risked a cautious word now and then, mostly among the women, with whom she'd be standing in the kitchen, who'd be giving little Anna milk to drink and all the time setting up their old lament, the usual complaint about their lives, punctuated with violent accusations, and infrequently a quick question, with a glance at the door to the living room —just to make sure: Who'll give a thought to us, ah, I don't believe a word of it, it's never happened yet, that's news to us . . .

There are people, Christa T. would say, who are interested in the news, and in new ideas, so you should do what you can about it. Driving home, the day's work done, they'd stop wherever she asked. They'd walk up a hill and look around; or go into an old church; or she'd ask Justus how the farms were managing, or he'd tell her stories about the farming people they'd just been to see. Probably she thought he was doing her a favor, and was even afraid of tiring him. But he'd never have learned about his area so quickly and thoroughly if it hadn't been for her questions. Once, when May had come and they could sit in the sun by the roadside—it wasn't exactly the most beautiful scene they were facing, in fact it was drab, except that it looked better in the light of this particular day—they both suddenly noticed they didn't want to leave the place. Neither said anything about it, but they knew it was what they were thinking.

I expect it was at about this time that they began to sketch plans for a house, as a game, no more than that. A game of the kind that can become an addiction.

Mother, says Anna when she has woken up one morning, now we look at one another like strangers! So soon? Christa T. thinks, won't believe it, pulls the child toward her, come on, let's have a cuddle, and as any mother would she quells the child's sense of strangeness by hugging Anna; but she doesn't have the illusion that she's hugging a part of herself. She lets the child go, and lets herself be looked at. Then they go out, across the fields, the footpath is hard and furrowed, it's summer. They take a rest on a patch of short grass surrounded by a low stone wall. Anna climbs up on a harrow and tugs at the gear lever, Christa T. sees her sitting up there with her legs dangling, a blue and green background behind her, luminous and dark. Then they have to run, a bank of clouds is coming up, but they can't make it. The rain pelts down at once with great force; after ten paces they're soaked to the skin. They rub one another's hair dry, sit down together on the long bench and drink hot cocoa; it's even darker now, hailstones are mixed with the rain. Mother, I'll tell you a story, says Anna. Telling lies is nice, isn't it?

During the evening, Christa T. tears a page from her household-accounts book. She writes: *Wind and sun. At one's back the town roofs in a barren reddish-gray row. The allotments with people digging and planting, squelching past one another on the narrow strips between freshly hoed ground. Beans there, cucumbers here, Aunt wants her carrots to go in there. Carefully the key is turned in the padlock on the wooden gate.* As opposed to this, the open dry footpath, the low wall, Anna on the harrow. Colors: red, blue, green, and one reads her meaning: *Sehnsucht* again, longing, and the craving to *see*. She manages to make this out of three colors. I shall always see the child sitting on the harrow, even if for her it was only a pretext, or because it was a pretext: the child is transparent and yet solid, precise without being paltry. If she wanted lastingness, she also wanted it to be felt that lastingness is transient.

The Story of the Washrag, which Anna tells her:

A yellow washrag with a red border, which had a mother just like everyone else, but suddenly the mother's heart wasn't beating much any more, so she was dead. So then the washrag has to bury his mother and do everything alone, even cooking. Of course he burns his fingers, and he can't put on a bandage all by himself, can't sit down at the table, can't find any candy in the cupboard, he can't do anything at all. So he flew out the window. The moon was shining, the owl was in the sky. A cat was walking past, it had an egg cup in each hand like the cats in Berlin. The owl flew to the lamp, the washrag followed it, but now along came an ashtray flying, with This Is A Bad Bad Ashtray written on it.

Then the washrag was frightened and flew to his mother. Then her heart started beating again, they walked home together and the mother made sure no more bad-bads came.

Nothing added, Christa T. writes, written down verbatim. Are all children poets?

She always has an urge to put down her pen, to listen to music, very old music or the latest. To fuel her dangerous wish for a pure and terrible perfection. To say all or nothing, and to hear, unmistakably, inside oneself the echo: nothing. Close the drawer, in which the scraps of paper are collecting. Everything half and half, a mess. No changing it. Waste of time. She's tired again, by early evening. During the last year this tiredness, which we sometimes discussed, must have become an overwhelming deathly weariness, and she resisted it ferociously. Her sickness came over her as tiredness, seductively. Christa T. must have suspected that it was a trap setting itself; and she decided not to grope her way into it. As always, when the record stopped, she stood up and made some strong coffee.

About this time Blasing usually arrived and she gave him a friendly welcome. He rubbed his hands, picked up the record: Something new?—drew his chair up to the little table: Your husband still inside the belly of some cow?

She knows him, for sure; she sees through him, but she's glad to be able to tell somebody that she's worrying. Three days ago Justus did his first operation on a cow due to calf soon, two nails and a big piece of glass in her paunch, he hasn't been home much. Everything looks all right; but what if this first operation of his went wrong?

Blasing is just the right person, considering the circumstances. Perhaps he's never really done anything in his life; but there's nothing he hasn't had a look at, one look at least. If you want, he'll draw on the table top a diagram of the inside of a cow due to calf soon, so that anyone can see that such an operation isn't a dangerous one at all, least of all

147

with Justus's talents. He himself, Blasing, has seen him bringing calves into the world; you can't tell Blasing there'll be any difficulties, not Blasing.

Christa T. has no wish to tell him anything, she listens to his brisk talk and suddenly all the things that have happened in all the villages of the district, which he knows better than anyone, have turned into handy little farces and jokes. Did the schoolteacher in B. try to kill herself? Well, if so, she made such a clumsy job of it that her fiancé couldn't help finding her, he's a cool bastard. —The bookkeeper of the cooperative in S. got two years? Well, what does that mean—his brother gets the job, doesn't he? And so who's lining whose pocket in the end, eh? —Old Willemers died of cirrhosis of the liver, did he? He knows better, Blasing does; the people at the hospital didn't notice the ruptured appendix, goddammit, what a world. Now they're covering up, all in the plot together.

Blasing made it sound as if everyone was plotting with everyone else and that was how it should be—if you didn't see the point, you had only yourself to blame. Was it true, Christa T. asked him, that he was getting a divorce, leaving his wife and three children . . . and that . . . ? Blasing raises his hands: What things people say! And thoughtfully he adds: Who knows what'll happen? Who knows where anyone can get on or off, or must—the trains keep coming and going. You don't think Blasing's going to let himself be got the better of, do you?

But here comes the boss.

Blasing starts to set up the chess pieces. Justus brings some wine. No chess. I'm worn out. The cow's all right. Come along tomorrow and have a look.

You see? Blasing says, now tell me who was right.

17

To become oneself, with all one's strength.

Difficult.

A bomb, a speech, a rifle shot—and the world can look a different place. And then where is this "self"?

A man like Blasing has seen through all the deceptions. He knows that it's not worth it, every time to pay with one's own being. All he can do is advise everyone to circulate faked currency. Nobody can prove anything and you can withdraw the currency at any time, quickly and painlessly: faked love, faked hatred, faked concern, and faked indifference. Besides, if you happen not to have noticed: the fake looks more genuine than the real thing because one can learn to regulate the doses as needed.

He thought it was up to him to calm Christa T., for she was now very restless. Time passes, Blasing, she told him;

and there wasn't anyone else she could tell. —That's all for the best, and if it didn't we'd have to force it to.

I really must come back to the day we spent on the Baltic coast. To the gigantic white and red ball which the wind was driving along. To her supple movements and to Justus's admiring looks and the way she tossed her head. To her smile, which I can certainly never describe, but also never forget. She had a dark tan and I said: This has been *your* summer. She laughed, white teeth and tanned face. Justus took her by the hair, which she wore short, and kissed her on the mouth in front of all the people. She took it all seriously, laughing all along. I can still see the look in her eyes.

That evening, when we were sitting in the seaside hotel, she wore a white dress—you can't imagine how old it is, she said, but she knew she could wear it for a long time yet. After a while she began to tot up figures on a beer mat, and when we asked what she was doing she said, gravely, and for the first time as far as we were concerned: It's the house. We must have raised our hands involuntarily, so she reeled off an explanation of the figures: Justus's monthly salary, the state subvention, the estimated cost, the mortgage rate, the time allowed for paying the mortgage. We looked at Justus. He admitted it was her idea and that at home she had whole writing pads full of plans. But who's going to make all the arrangements, we asked, it's so difficult nowadays.

Me, said Christa T.

She pulled some plans from her handbag and spread them on the round, marble-topped table. For the first time we saw "the house": all its levels, its rooms, every wall and every step of every stairway. Then we saw that it was already in existence and that nobody had any right to push it back into nonexistence.

But where is it, we asked. Christa T. produced a large map of the area. She ran her brown index finger along the road. It goes as far as here, she said. She turned down a farm road: here it's bad. Then came a village: here the surface is terrible. The last stretch, up the hill, was really catastrophic.

But when you've got there you suddenly see the lake. Startles you. The lake, enormous, lonely, nothing but meadows and trees to right and left, and potato fields behind you. Poplars grow along the shore, they grow quickly and act as a windbreak, and imagine how the wind blows there in winter! We shall need thick plate glass on the lake side of the house, two huge windows. From the kitchen I can see the garden I'm laying out, and the western tip of the lake. We can cook with propane gas; Justus can always change the bottles in town. A stretch of the shore is being cleared of reeds: we can swim from there. Anna and Lena can run around stark naked in the summer.

I can do the job almost on my own, then the house will be all set. The architect draws up the plans as I tell him.

You've had plenty of practice building houses, we said, there's not much left to be done, if you know every nail . . .

Every nail and every stage; I've already woken up there in the mornings sometimes, believe it or not.

But we had scruples about owning a house: property owners! we said, wrinkling our noses. I said to her quietly: But you'll be burying yourself.

She smiled and said: No, I'm digging my way out.

I didn't quite understand that.

None of us was superstitious, nobody touched wood, nobody told her to keep her impatient dreams to herself, to bridle her daydreams and not count her chickens. We drank a bottle of wine to the house, then another. My God, what a lovely white house it was, on the hill by the lake, my God, how well the reed thatch suits it, what fine proportions, not too big and not too small, and how practical, perfect in its way, and what a beautiful position, right in the middle of the old cattle-breeding region, Justus was already stepping up the milk production.

Suddenly we all saw it standing there, her house, we saw

that someone had had to think it out, and now it was there, it existed. She had invented it: we all clinked glasses with her.

Christa T. drank more than usual, she was asked to dance by people from the next table, everyone had seen us pushing and pulling the plans about, people had come up with warnings and words of advice, giving addresses of work-men, and Christa T. was grateful for all of it. She danced with everyone, finally even with the dumpy income-tax official, who'd seen more than one farmer start daring and proud and end shamefaced and humble in his office.

The house was built. But one can count the nights she slept under its roof.

The poplars were planted. They've grown so well that Justus recently had to consider pollarding the ones in front of the windows.

The lake is there, calm and smooth in summer, wild in autumn, white and frozen in winter. I've seen the sun set in it as she stood beside me.

The reeds by the shore have been cut and in summer the three children swim there every day. They run around naked, not many people wander into these parts.

From the kitchen window I've seen her garden and the western tip of the lake. The kitchen was chaos, because after his wife's death Justus hadn't been able to find a house-keeper and hardly had time to keep it tidy by himself. While I was putting the dishes away I recognized the ar-rangement of the cupboards and shelves that she'd thought out. I slept behind the flowered curtains she had chosen for the alcoves in the upstairs rooms. In the night I woke and heard the rats scuttling overhead in the attic. We put some stuff down to get rid of them and they've gone now.

The next morning, as I was standing by the wall of books in the big living room taking out the books I'd sent Christa T. in the hospital, I thought I felt a sudden chill in the air, and it was as if a shadow had fallen across my shoulders. I had to keep myself from swinging around to catch her by surprise, sitting there in her chair, with her face turned away from me, for in the last months she always turned away and wouldn't let anyone photograph her as she sat there in her thick green woollen cardigan, though it was summer. She got cold so easily.

I drew myself up stiff and didn't turn round, at least not right away; and when I did turn she wasn't there, and no shadow had fallen, and there's no photo of her from the last months.

The children, hers and mine, were shouting outside. A rabbit had made its burrow under the house, and they wanted to catch it and take it somewhere else.

I went to the door.

The area for the terrace still needed cementing; everywhere work had been left half finished. I walked outside. Suddenly I realized that to this moment I hadn't understood why she wanted to live here and why she'd built the house. I was more surprised than perplexed at this, for now it was perfectly clear, and it was surprising that this house should be nothing but a sort of instrument that she meant to use to link herself more intimately with life, a place with which she was profoundly familiar because she had created it herself and on whose territory she could take her stand against anything alien.

Security, yes, that too.

Now that no judgment of mine could change anything, because all judgments were obsolete and superfluous, I asked myself what other kind of life I could have advised her to live. And as often as I've thought about this since then—I can see no better life for her than the one she chose herself. I know that a small work place was planned for her at one of the big windows. Perhaps, she once said, perhaps at that desk I'll be able to get the better of this accursed sloth of mine. —That's what she called it.

As is so often the case, the physical difficulties in the way of her plan hid what it really meant, even from her. It was costing more than they'd anticipated and there often seemed no prospect of getting the most basic materials, to keep the work moving at least. When, during these two years, they came to take a breather at our place, they'd be coming from the design center, where they'd been hoping to find lamps or furniture or door handles. They were always in a hurry, always fearful that the whole project would grind to a halt. One evening when we took them to their car, I thought Christa T. was more disheartened than was warranted by the troubles she'd complained of. I said something to cheer her up. Justus, who was standing behind her, nodded imploringly and meaningfully at me, I gave him a questioning look, and Christa T. eluded all sympathy with an airy remark. I didn't know what was going on. They got into the car, we made a date for them to come again and so put off any real conversation till the next time. They drove away.

It hadn't been enough to give one any presentiments. One seldom does try to understand really what one sees or hears, what another person says or doesn't say. Weeks later when she called me up—a thing she never did, usually—I was surprised and delighted. Only after we'd been talking for a whole minute and had said all the essentials about our work and the children, and after there'd been a sudden silence, only then did I ask myself: what's it all about?

I can recall exactly how she put it: I'm being very foolish, she said.

Are you alone? I asked—very quietly, I couldn't help myself—as if I knew what follies she wanted to tell me about.

Yes, she said.

Here my recollection of her exact words stops, and I don't think I should invent them. She told me that she had—fallen in love with another man (was that how she put it? what else could she have said?). A hunting friend of Justus.

Well, that's all there is to it.

No, there's a bit more: the thing—that's what she said—the thing's getting out of hand.

I recall thinking I suddenly understood what it was I'd

noticed about her recently, but I didn't want to believe it. I said, quickly: Madame Bovary.

That was no news to her, but what use was it? Did she just want to talk, at last to be able to talk, or did she really want to know what I thought? Whatever it was, I told her: You must put an end to it, these things never do anyone any good . . .

But what's an end in such affairs? And how should one do what one should but can't do?

Does Justus know?

Of course.

Now I really did get worried. Krischan, I said, I don't know what you want of me. I can only tell you this: it's wrong.

Why? she asked, defiantly. Do you think I'm made to be faithful?

I saw that she was lumping me together with other people, simply out of a desire to be unjust—with what other people? Justus?—but all I said was: Yes, that's what you're made to be.

She didn't say anything for a while; then abruptly she said: I know. —In a way which suggested she alone could know about that.

The silences kept getting longer. Eventually she said something about not knowing what to do, couldn't help it, and she quickly hung up.

When it happens, we've known it all mostly before; I don't think she was surprised at herself. One's only surprised when other people say: Oh, it's the usual thing.

It was Justus who'd brought him into their home, a young forester. The seduction, if any, was at her initiative: he's never met a woman like this before. He reacts quite ingenuously, and couldn't have done better if he'd been following some crafty plan. At the hunt dance, when they're dancing together, he embraces her; the next day he sends her a rabbit. He leaps at a chance to look at her bird books. Quietly, when the children are asleep, he imitates the calls of birds. He puts his hand on her shoulder. After this she'll sometimes stand for an hour by the window, when she thinks he might pass by. When he does come, walking under her window, when he looks up and doffs his hat, she has to hold on tight to the window seat. She has to sit down and put her hands over her face. She's startled to find her hands so cold and her face so hot.

She'd like to wish it was all over, but she can't; how can one wish life to be over? She understands when Justus goes wild with disappointment and helplessness; he can rage, knock over the table; can run off and come home late at night; she notices he's been drinking. Then for days he can say nothing. But all she can do is look at him and then, when he's left again, lapse once more into her boundless and dangerous fantasies. She hasn't tried to explain or gloss over or regret anything. Sometimes when she comes to herself again after a bout of deep reverie, she may ask herself: am I sick? It seems surprising to her that everyone who was close to her has now become a stranger; but why surprising? After all, hasn't she become a stranger to herself?

"Madame Bovary" was missing the point, I know it. There would be no paltry dealings, no attempts to deceive, and no tactics of evasion. She'd be more likely to destroy herself than . . . But that was why I was scared.

Many more feelings when I wake in the morning than can be used up during the day: this is one of the few notes she wrote down at that time. The unused feelings begin to poison her. For the first time she asks herself what in all the world she was wanting this house for, what had she talked herself into, what was she going to make now of this half-botched life of hers. She'd forgotten everything; could think of nothing to console or encourage herself. She couldn't ask Justus, during those weeks he wasn't there for her, he was fighting for his own existence. Some money had been embezzled at one of the cooperatives; there were signs of negligence in the tending of the cattle; the shifty director tried to implicate the inexperienced young vet and so Justus had to go on the witness stand at the court of inquiry, he sensed mistrust all around, believed everyone thought him slovenly and incompetent. He nursed his grievance, drank alone in a bar that evening, got back into his car all the same, and drove slowly and carefully through the town, was stopped, checked, and given a ticket.

A bad time, he said to me, I simply couldn't talk to her about my problems. I didn't want her to see me the way I was seeing myself. Only I was surprised when she took the car sometimes and drove wildly around the country for hours, and when she came back she was dead tired.

Christa T. walked around in her home like a caged animal. She knew she'd thought every thought a million times over, that every single feeling was worn down to the core by overuse, and that every one of her handy household skills could be done just as well by anyone else. All her attempts to break out of the dead center in which she'd planted herself rebounded at her with a terrible indifference. She felt the secret that made her life livable was relentlessly escaping from her: the consciousness of who she really was. She saw herself melting away in an endless welter of deadly banal actions and clichés.

Anything would do, as long as it told her something new about herself. She had to know there was still some sense in her sensations, that it wasn't utterly pointless to go on seeing and hearing, tasting and smelling things. So she hit on this young man, who looked up to her as to some kind of apparition, who held her in his arms, who put his hand on her shoulder. Then she felt the life coming back into her, even if only as pain; and simply to pass a teacup across the table made her suddenly herself again.

If she had lived, this wouldn't be the last proof that she couldn't cope with the *données* of life. I was afraid of the price she was paying, and perhaps I privately called it misery and misfortune, not taking into account the fact that misfortune can be a reasonable price to pay for refusing assent. We had still seemed like characters in a well-made play, the end of which would infallibly be the dissolution of all complications and conflicts, so that every one of the moves we made, whether of our own will or under pressure, would eventually find its justification in terms of the end. Christa T. must at that time have been tumbling out of the hands of this utterly amiable but very banal playwright. She must suddenly have contemplated a bad end, or at least a disorderly one; something must have incited her to try out moves of the kind that lead precisely nowhere.

So it had to be this forbidden love, or whatever you want to call it. Let's see how he knocks over the table, let's see what the faces look like when this sort of thing happens. Let's see how my own face looks when everything's called into question again.

They weren't her choosing, the circumstances and occasions which enabled her to play once more with the few things she really had a hold on, and once more to raise the stakes.

When that happens, all one's calculations naturally lose force, and one goes into a swoon.

18

When I saw her again this "matter" was hardly mentioned any more and there was no bitterness left in her, nothing of this dangerous, objectless craving either. She was standing by the stove, dealing with the pots and pans, and suddenly she said that she was expecting again, with a slight undertone of triumph in her voice, which I think I didn't misinterpret. So that's how you solve your problems, I said, and we laughed.

It was then, during our last visit to her old home, at New Year's 1961–2, that she showed me the curtain material, the new set of dishes, and the colorful plastic canisters for the kitchen, which pleased her especially. Her rooms were full of baskets and boxes, we sat on the floor and scattered the new things around us. She wanted to start afresh; there weren't going to be any of the old things in the new house.

In the afternoon we saw the house for the first time. Silent with anticipation we turned off the main road, took the farm road, bumped through the village—worst cooperative in the district, said Justus—and worked our way up the miserable hill road.

Then there it was, naked and raw, very much alone beneath the huge cloudy sky, and smaller than we'd pictured it. It looked as if it needed help in its battle with the big turbulent lake and the dark sky. We saw that it was standing its ground bravely, but also that nature was against it; but we didn't say anything about this. We crossed the rough plank which served as a threshold into the interior of the house, walked slowly through the downstairs rooms, still without floorboards, and climbed a ladder to reach the upper floor, the children's bedrooms. A strong wind was blowing through all the cracks. This wind of yours is just as you said, we told Christa T., leaving it an open question whether we found everything else likewise. But she couldn't be shaken. She knew quite well that this raw house with the wind whistling through it was further from completion than the dream house on the plans that happy evening at the seaside hotel, the white and beautiful house on the pieces of paper. But she'd also learned that real materials are more resistant than paper, and that, as long as things are still in the process of coming to be, one has to drive them tenaciously along. We saw that she no longer insisted on her sketches, but on these raw stones. We stood around the cold fireplace and discussed what kind of decor would suit it best, argued about styles and varieties of stone, and quietly doubted—as one always does doubt, especially right near the end—whether we'd ever eat a meal cooked in the kitchen of this house.

But our doubts were petty and we've eaten the meal. Seven months later, at the end of July, we were all sitting around the big circular table. The unruffled shining lake almost came into the room through the window, the door to the patch for the lawn was open, the tops of the slender poplar saplings sparkled, and out of the kitchen came Christa T., now cumbrous and heavy, with a big bowl of spiced potatoes.

It was one of the moments at which one fears the envy of the gods, but I secretly offered them an exchange: the fright we'd got when we arrived, they should be satisfied with that and not seek vengeance, bridle their destructiveness. Be content with what they'd already contrived.

I don't know if she noticed anything in my face. When we were alone for a moment, she said—as if to steal a march on me: I've gotten older.

I passed over the question this remark implied, answered evasively, and thought to myself that "older" wasn't the right word—although one might have spoken of her becoming older if the changes affecting her had taken seven years and not a trifling seven months. Her face was puffy, her skin rough and scaly, and the veins stood out on her arms and legs.

I supposed it was all because of her pregnancy, but she shook her head. She named a medicine she'd been taking; oddly enough I still recall the name. Prednisone, she said, in large doses. It was the only remedy. It meant one had to put up with certain other troubles.

She meant it, and she knew what she meant. We others were set apart from her by our not having had a certain experience; we hadn't caught up with her, you might say. An experience which one can only have directly and personally, not vicariously, and in which nobody else can share. We knew that it was as inept to feel embarrassed as it was to feel guilty. But how can one react appropriately to the experience of death?

When we went for a swim we kept telling her to take things easy, but she paid no attention. She dropped her beach robe on the shore and waded rapidly through the shallow, weed-green water to the deeper level where one can swim. She called to me to follow her, so that I shouldn't get caught among the weeds and tendrils. She wanted to

introduce me to her lake. We swam along beside one another, I let her set the pace and before long I pretended I
was tired. She didn't believe me; one had to be careful not
to let her notice one was trying to spare her.

Justus hinted that I should give her a talking-to. She'd
worked for hours hoeing weeds the day before in the garden; she worked like mad and had no regard for her—condition. An ambiguous word, we both noticed; but he said
no more. I didn't take the opportunity to ask what prospects
the doctors had offered. We stood by the tacit agreement not
to talk about her behind her back. We were like people who
are afraid that if they breathe a single word the ground
they're standing on will disintegrate.

After lunch we persuaded her to lie down, and we drove
with Justus to the old tumble-down inn where eels from the
fish cooperative were smoked. He bought a large one,
wrapped in newspaper. He introduced us to the pets, an old
dog, half blind, and a wildish mistrustful cat, for which he'd
brought a cure for mange. On the way back we discussed
what might be made of this place if it got into the right
hands; a popular resort for excursionists, said Justus, a gold
mine. But I hope they won't clutter the whole place with
cars and motorboats . . . I can only remember the inn and
the animals and our conversation because I wasn't forgetting we all knew we should really be talking about something else; but that wasn't possible.

Not until evening . . .

But that July evening doesn't belong here. What does is
that New Year's evening, and before it the return from our
visit to the house, the return during which the snowstorm
began. Justus had to stop in one of the villages to have a
small repair job done on his car. The mechanic knew him
and made every effort to help him quickly. We got out of
the car and stood in a corner, out of the wind. Christa T.
told me stories about her children; and it struck me that,
unlike other mothers, she didn't notice only the flattering
episodes and enjoyable moments: she was incorruptible. A

few days before, Anna and her little sister hand in hand had followed a funeral procession and had been stopped only at the last moment from going right up to the graveside.

She was wild with excitement, said Christa T.: I explained to her that only close relatives are allowed to be there when a person is buried. Then she said to me: Oh, please die soon, I want to see how you're buried!

But then you won't see me again.

I know, Anna said calmly.

She's so factual, Christa T. said, without a trace of affectation. —I've never known a mother who tried less to mold her children in her own image. When she died and her death was being concealed from Anna, I sometimes thought of our conversation at the repair shop; and if I hadn't found a verbatim record of a dialogue with Anna among Christa T.'s papers, I'd have been hesitant about putting it down here, because we usually ascribe to the silliest casual events an ominous and somber meaning, at least if things have a somber end.

There were no dark omens at that New Year's Eve celebration.

We all remember it, even Blasing, who doesn't often recollect anything unless there's a story in it for him to sell. Even he remembers, I know, because he told me so when I met him recently in Berlin. As usual, he was hugging his black briefcase containing a manuscript, or the makings of one; and he was "doing the rounds," as he called it, offering his wares. He was wearing a new overcoat, which suited him well, and he indulged himself in a little mournfulness. Yes, he said, of our New Year celebration, that was one of the last happy evenings, and after it life began to get serious, who could have predicted it? He presumably meant that one year after it he actually did get a divorce and move to Berlin to begin his career, I realized all this. But I was surprised that he should call the celebration, in his memory of it, "happy." And it perplexed me even more that he genuinely meant it. Even though he didn't as usual go on about meaning it "in all due seriousness" as he would say. He'd now brought his vocabulary up to city standards. All the same, he finally said, even after we'd said goodbye: She was a rare person. And I nodded because he then got embarrassed and because he'd never say such a thing in the offices of the publishers who took his manuscripts.

Günter had also traveled over, and I can't believe that Christa T. was really so surprised as she pretended to be. It turned out that Günter was still unmarried and that there was still a close bond between him and Christa T.

Don't be jealous without reason, she said to Justus, the way you tend to be.

See how she is? Justus said to us, that's her all over.

They could laugh about themselves; Christa T. was on top of the world. Everyone was so friendly to Günter that he didn't know what it was all about; and several times he was on the verge of making sure that the good mood we were in was not his doing. He was now the principal at the school in his home town.

We must watch him a bit, Christa T. told me, he'll be picking a quarrel with Blasing.

The quarrel never really materialized, although I feel as if it had. One or two years later it would have been unavoidable; but it hadn't yet reached that point. Christa T. had simply seen it coming. She was now a woman who managed a household, invited guests, and saw to it that they didn't fight. What's become of us all, we thought. Our astonishment made us feel gentle; one could be gentle without becoming sentimental. Suddenly it was fun to decorate the table, straighten the mats, light the candles. The windows, with the wind sweeping gusts of snow against them, were hung with blankets. In came Christa T., carrying a dish with roasted cuts of wild boar on it.

But I shouldn't give the impression that it was all because of the candles and the wine and the cuts of wild boar; it was something else, and it's not easy to describe. Nonetheless, I'd be inclined to say that such a gathering, in such a spirit, couldn't occur again, because this floating equipoise which we all felt like a slight drunkenness couldn't easily be repeated. It has to do with frankness and a harmless form of self-exaltation; and above all one can't produce it deliberately. We took it as our reward, simply that; and so it stayed, for we all believed the worst times were now behind us, the worst in ourselves too; we were so certain that our examinations in life would eventually be certified "passed."

We began to reminisce. We suddenly found—not one of us over thirty-five—that we had something you might call a past. But our understanding was that general concerns can't prejudice the individual. The women were showing pictures around: Good Lord, these curls, these long sack dresses, these little combs in our hair! And how serious we were! We laughed at our old seriousness.

Do you remember, Christa T. said to Günter, the time you tried to prove to Frau Mrosow that the fate of Schiller's Luise can still concern us all? I was scared that Christa T. might have gone too far, for I was certain that Günter had never once spoken to anyone about that time, about Inge, about Kostia and his own unhappy love affair. But now he only nodded and smiled; Christa T. always managed to find the right moment to talk about something that would have been too painful a day earlier and merely boring a day later. Yes, Günter said, I can still see myself standing there, I really did go off the deep end.

So now that too was a thing of the past. Günter raised his glass and drank to Christa T. She blushed, but she didn't act bashful; and all at once we understood everything, and were a little touched; and we didn't conceal the fact that we understood. We all drank to her—or I very much wish we had—to her with whom everyone of us had a firm relationship and a different kind of relationship, and who managed to cope with all these relationships shrewdly and generously and above all without calculation.

If everything was as I now wish it to have been, we found it quite natural that there should be, at the back of all these relationships, something like an awkward love or old-fashioned admiration. If we all behaved that evening as I now wish we had, we were all generous and wanted to miss no feeling and no nuance of feeling; for to all of it, we might have thought, we were entitled. All that evening, New Year's Eve 1961–2, her last but one, Christa T. was setting us, I say, an example—setting it for the infinite possibilities still in us.

She knew this and she wasn't being bashful about it.

Inevitably we began to tell stories, the kind that rise up in one's mind when the floods recede. One's a little surprised that these stories are all that's left; and one feels obliged to touch them up a bit, inserting a moral and shaping the end, above all, whatever one may think about it, to one's own advantage. It's not difficult if one is so firmly convinced that the end really will turn out to one's advantage and that the many small ends will quietly subordinate themselves to the big one. Briefly, we were telling tall stories, working to create a past one can tell one's children about: after all, the time was ripe.

The quarrel, as I said, didn't materialize. What put the idea into Christa T.'s head? For naturally Günter's stories were very different from Blasing's, the latter subjecting himself continuously to correction by his wife, until we all noticed that he really didn't care how he got his effects as long as people laughed, as long as he was a success.

You, Christa T. suddenly said—so it wasn't Günter after all, it was she! —You, Blasing, that's all very old hat what you're telling us. Why not tell us about this evening? About ourselves.

First, Blasing took a long swallow of his drink, then he said: What could be simpler? Once upon a time . . .

He did it quite well. He'd detected everyone's weak points, also our better points, he didn't spare himself either, and only right at the end did we notice that he'd put us all into tins long prepared and even labeled to receive us, tins in existence perhaps even before we were born. All Blasing had to do was clap the lids on, and now we'd been dealt with, we knew all about ourselves and nobody had the slightest reason to stir a finger or make a single move. Nobody had any reason to go on living, and Frau Blasing, who ran a grocery store and was bringing up her three children, told her husband bluntly she'd always suspected he wanted to kill her.

It was all in fun and what was there to quarrel about? Yet I couldn't help thinking back on it briefly when I met Blasing the other day with his black briefcase. Günter would certainly have inquired about his manuscripts; he always asks people insistently about their work. He'd have read whatever Blasing gave him, even right there in the middle of the Friedrichstrasse, and then they really would have quarreled. But at that time, New Year's Eve 1961-2, we still weren't so sure. We talked about Blasing, after he'd left, a thing one shouldn't do. We wondered if he'd have any of the success he longed for. Günter disagreed with Christa T., who said: He's bluffing, but he won't last.

Günter said: He wants everything to be fixed and definite. He can't help it. Even if it means cutting off heads to make people stand still for him . . . But by then he wasn't talking about Blasing any more.

Then we heard Christa T. talking about her difficulties— the only time she ever did so. We were all tired, and we'd been drinking; next morning one can forget everything one's heard at 3 a.m. Christa T. said she didn't like things to be fixed: that everything, once it's out there in existence —even this phrase which puts it out there—is so difficult to get moving again, so one should try in advance to keep it alive while it's still in the process of coming to be, in oneself. It must keep on *originating,* that's what matters. One should never, never let it become something finished.

But how can anyone do this?

19

The year is over. The law comes into effect which reminds us to let it go, and we have to abide by that law. Just this one scene, though, which comes up out of memory with such difficulty.

Writing means making things large.

Did she say this, or is memory playing me false? For every statement one needs the place where it was uttered and the moment to match it.

Small and petty things, she says, can take care of themselves.

Yes: twilight. I know: morning twilight. The smell of cigarette smoke which must have awakened me. The wall of books on which my glance first falls and which I can't immediately recognize. She's sitting there at the roll-top desk, which is covered with Justus's papers, in her faded red dressing gown, and she's writing: The Big Hope, or The Difficulty of Saying "I."

When I got up I saw the sheet of paper there with my own eyes; but now it has disappeared. Writing means making things large. Yes, it's possibly so: she didn't say it, I read it.

Not disturbing you, am I? she says. Go on sleeping, if you like.

I'm disinclined to believe that I really was asleep. Even if up to this moment I'd forgotten that morning, as one commonly forgets dreams. Even if it makes me mistrustful, coming back to me just now in all clarity and certainty, appearing the way only the most desirable inventions do.

She'd certainly agree to that: for she knew the power that inventions have over us. That morning, the first of the New Year, when she was so wide awake and I was so sleepy, we might have talked about many things, but my mind was too much at rest. I was cradled in the certainty that much was still reversible and attainable, as long as one didn't lose patience and faith in oneself. An untidy confidence had me in its clutches; I believed that all would be well. Only her face, as she leaned over the sheet of paper, seemed strange. Yes, I said—the way one says things, between sleeping and waking, which one doesn't ordinarily say: the same face. I once saw you blowing a trumpet, eighteen years ago.

Curious, she seemed to know.

Her secret, which I'd been looking for all the time we'd known one another, was a secret no longer. What she wanted, in her innermost depths, what she dreamed of and what she'd long ago begun to do, now lay open before me, incontestable and beyond the shadow of a doubt. It seems to me now that we'd known it all along. She certainly hadn't kept the secret fearfully, it was just that she hadn't intruded upon it. Her long hesitation, her experiments with various forms of living, her amateurishness in various realms, all these pointed in the same direction, if only you had the eyes to see. She was trying out the possibilities of life until nothing should be left: that much was understandable.

Among her papers are various fragments written in the third person: *she,* with whom she associated herself, whom she was careful not to name, for what name could she have given her? *She,* who knows she must always be new, and see anew, over and over again; and who can do what she must wish to do. *She,* who knows only the present and won't let herself be deprived of the right to live according to the laws of her own being.

I understand the secret of the third person, who is there without being tangible and who, when circumstances favor her, can bring down more reality upon herself than the first person: I. The difficulty of saying "I."

Was I really asleep? I saw her go by, in all her forms; saw suddenly behind all her transformations the meaning; understood that it's inept to wish for her to arrive and stay anywhere. And I say something to this effect in half sleep. Anyway, she smiles, smokes her cigarette, and writes.

Everything takes a terribly long time with me, she says; but by now we're standing in the small village shop where Justus is having his car repaired, and the wind sweeps through the half-open door, and we ask ourselves at the same moment what this monotonous hammering in the corner and this howling of the wind have to do with our conversation, which concerns time, for I find we haven't got as much time as she takes. But she's suddenly more distinct than she ever was before; and to all of us she gives time for the taking, as long as we know what it's for.

And you know?

She smiles. Go on sleeping, she says.

Then I'm not tired any more either. We walk through the town—red row of barns, church, pharmacy, store, café. It's evening, cold. We're carrying string bags with bottles in them. We look through the windows of the houses we're passing. She knows how the people live who are sitting there beneath the small colored dim standard lamps that have become fashionable in recent years. She knows the taste of the sauté potatoes which are eaten here in the evenings. She understands what the women unwittingly reveal to her, the women who are now closing their doors for the start of the New Year holiday. She tells me stories which are curiously true, although they don't actually happen; but her heroes have the name of the family now gathering before our eyes beneath the electric candles on the Christmas tree, to eat blood sausage and sauerkraut. Christa T. swears that behind the smooth satisfied faces of the parents, of the little boy and the big girl, lurk exactly the same thoughts as the ones which she, in her story, is turning into deeds.

Write, Krischan, why don't you write? —Oh well, she says, well, you know . . .

She was afraid of the imprecision and ineptness of words. She knew that they do harm, the insidious harm of bypassing life, which she fears almost more than the great catastrophes. She thought life can be wounded by what one says. I know this from Kostia's letter: she must have confessed as much to him, and he alludes to it, having himself now left the irresponsible realm of a merely verbal existence.

We're walking up the stairs to her house, have turned the key in the lock, can hear jazz in the living room and Anna singing softly in the kitchen. As a matter of fact, Christa T. says, perhaps there are one or two things I've got in mind.

I ask Justus.

Yes, he says. I know. She means her sketches. "Around the Lake," she called them. The lake by our house. The villages around. Their story. She visited the local church archives and looked at their documents. It was to be the life of the present, sharply outlined against the background of history. The peasants told her everything, I don't know how she got them to. You should have seen her at the cooperative dance; it was just before she had to go away. She didn't refuse a single dance, but during the intervals she sat at the bar and drew them out—she had the stories coming out of their ears. They didn't need to be asked, because they saw that she wasn't putting them on or acting up but really did almost fall off her stool from laughing when they told her about the gravedigger Hinrichsen's wedding. She made notes; you'll find them.

I didn't find them. Also I didn't find the sheet of paper she'd been writing on that strange morning, which I'd looked at when she was called away by the children and I got up. What I saw wasn't a continuous text, to be sure, only a few notes, and I couldn't figure out the connections. After the curious sentence about the difficulty of saying "I," came the words: "Facts! Stick to the facts." And underneath, in brackets: *But what are facts?*

Facts are the traces left in us by events. That was her view, Gertrud Born says, now Gertrud Dölling. She felt more and more certain about it, I know, the more she thought about it. You see, she was one-sided, of course she was.

Why of course, Gertrud Born?

Then she looks at me as if I didn't understand the simplest things. How could everything that happens become a fact for each individual person? She simply sought out the facts that suited her best—as everyone does, she quietly said. Another thing: she had a craving for honesty.

O la la, says Blasing, and he even wags a menacing finger: our eternal dreamer! It was Blasing himself who suggested the game we played that New Year's night between two and three in the morning, when nobody was taking things seriously any more. First he asked the question: what is indispensable for the survival of mankind? Each person wrote his answer on the back of one of Justus's milk-quota forms, folded it and passed it to the next person.

I know her handwriting and afterwards I looked to see what her answer was. Conscience—there it was in her handwriting. Imagination.

It was then that Blasing wagged his finger. O la la, she'd taken it seriously; but she wasn't going to justify herself. She also didn't deny that the exploitation of all the earth's energy resources . . . No, who'd contradict Blasing on such a point?

Günter walks up to him. Günter sitting with us on the stairs at the university, it's nighttime, a fragrance from the lime trees, what are the lime trees doing here? The order of things is finally falling apart. What I'd like is a little more order, I say, and a little more vision. Then she looks across to me as I lie sleeping there, laughs again, but says quite seriously: Me too.

If only one could believe you mean it, says Günter anxiously, who can tell what you're up to? Then she's astonished, you can see it in her eyes, which withdraw while we go on talking and talking. The puny ego, we say scornfully, sitting on our stairs. The old Adam, we've finished him off. She says nothing, thinks, thinks, I now know, for years on end until finally, one night in our loggia in Berlin, with the S-Bahn trains thundering by, she says what she thinks: I really don't know. There must be some misunderstanding. All this trouble, just to make sure that every one of us gets to be different—and all so as to get rid of that difference in time too?

I can't accept that, she says, I can't believe in it. Why not? Because one can decide, in certain realms, to regard one thing as true and another as false. Just as people decided, at some time or other, to believe in the good nature of man, because it was helpful to believe it, as a working hypothesis.

Then she talked to me about her students. We were walking from the Marx-Engels Platz to the Alexanderplatz. We stood by the newsstand and let the hundreds of faces go by; we bought the last anemones at the flower shop. Perhaps we're a bit drunk with springtime, I said. But she insisted she was sober and that she knew what she was saying. She said we had a right to invent, to think out inventions that should be audacious but never careless.

Because nothing can become reality unless it has been thought out beforehand.

She was all for reality, that's why she loved the time when real changes were being made. She loved to open up new senses for the sense of a new thing: she wanted to teach her students to be valuable to themselves. I know that she once lost control when one of them looked at her with big eyes and innocently asked: Why? She kept coming back to this: the fact that she hadn't been able to give an answer tormented her for a long time. Was she thinking of this when she wrote, that morning, while I slept, on her piece of paper: *The goal—fullness. Joy. Hard to put a name to it.*

Nothing could be more inappropriate than pity or regret. She did live. She was all there. She was always scared of getting stuck; her shyness and her timidity were the reverse side of her passion for wishing. Now out she came, calm even in the unfulfillment of her wishes, for she had the strength to say: Not yet. She carried many lives around with her, storing them in herself; and in herself she stored many times as well, times in which she lived partially unknown, as was the case in her "real" time; and what is not possible in one time becomes real in another. But she called all her various times, serenely: Our time.

Writing means making things large. Pulling ourselves together, let's see her writ large. One's wishes are only what one is capable of. Thus her deep and persistent wish guarantees the secret existence of her work: this *long and never-ending journey toward oneself.*

The difficulty of saying "I."

If I were to have to invent her, I wouldn't change her. I'd let her live, among ourselves, whom she, with uncommon knowing, chose as her companions in life. I'd let her sit at the desk, one morning in the twilight, noting the experiences into which the facts of real life had crystallized in her. I'd let her stand up when the children called. Not quench the thirst she always feels. Give her, when she needs it, confidence that her strength was still on the increase; she needed nothing more. I'd gather around her people who were important to her. I'd let her finish the few pages she wanted to leave us, and which, unless we're not utterly deceived, would have been news from the inmost being, that deepest level of being which is harder to reach than the underside of the earth's crust, harder to reach than the stratosphere, because it is more safely guarded: by each one of us.

I'd have let her live.

So that I could sit, as I did that morning, again and again at her table. For Justus who's bringing the coffee pot in, for the children who are speechless with joy because their favorite pastries are on their plates.

Then the sun rose, red and cold. There was snow on the ground. We took our time over breakfast. Stay a while, Christa T. said; but we drove off.

If I'd been allowed to invent us, I'd have given us time to stay.

20

Now comes her death. It takes a year, and then it is done with; it leaves no doubts that it has done everything possible; it isn't averse to fixing and defining things, for that's what it needs to do. So nothing much can be said about it.

But we must speak of her dying.

It announces itself with an exasperating increase of her tiredness, which attracted no attention at first. Incredibly tired, she says. The doctor gives her stimulants. Deathly tired, tired to death. I can't even get up the stairs any more. —But what does this "can't any more" mean? —And just now that we're getting ready to move . . . Yes, and what does this mean, "now"?

One afternoon she faints. Justus finds her leaning against the wall, sitting on the clothes chest. It is March, two weeks before they're due to move.

After the first examination at the hospital they say: too

late. The hemoglobin content in the blood has gone beyond the danger limit. We can't do anything.

After the blood transfusion a vague consciousness returns, easily blurring again. She knew she was being taken somewhere. Where are we going, she murmured. —Since she has crossed the limit, other laws apply; in the country where she now is, people speak untruths in hushed voices: Don't worry, Krischan. They'll look after you better in G.

She can't smile, but she wants to show concern; her weakness isn't yet such that she loses all regard for other people.

What a nuisance I am, she says. Then she loses consciousness again.

The doctors in G. have been notified about the state she's in. She's rolled into the death room. My God, the nurse says, and such a young woman too. And in her condition . . .

When she really did die a year later, they didn't put her in the death room. Justus thought she might recognize it, if she regained consciousness. So they just put a screen around her bed.

At first she isn't afraid; she hasn't the strength to be conscious of any danger. "Hovering between life and death" is a good expression; truly one can only picture a stay in that realm as a state of hovering. Presumably the shadows of death are there, likewise only very indistinct colors, forms, sounds, and smells. One can't see or hear; but pain stops, and fear too. Outlines are blurred. One's own outlines seem to expand; but, as in certain dreams, one doesn't stand out clearly against one's background any more. Everything liquefies, there's an interchanging of the elements, and one can feel it happening, perhaps one can even retain a vague memory of it, it's astonishing, it makes curious motions, but it isn't entirely unfamiliar: how can this be explained? This memory won't be permanent, and it certainly won't be frightening.

The fear comes with consciousness, as a shock. Am I very

sick, one can ask the nurse when one wakes up. No doubt she'll answer: Certainly not, what can you be thinking of?

But she doesn't say it. What she says is: We can do wonders sometimes, I've seen a few myself.

Then the doctors are standing around the bed, Latin words floating back and forth; they're relying rather too much on the dim state of the patient's consciousness, so during their excited argument they utter the word she shouldn't hear: leukemia.

Is it that, doctor? Tell me the truth, I want to know the truth.

Certainly not, what can you be thinking of?

If the truth does look as it seems to look, then one can get on without it. Then she'd prefer to hear what they're willing to tell her, though somewhat too diffusely—about the dangerous and harmless variants of every disease, about diseases which are intractable at the start but amenable to discussion, so that one can watch them, outwit them, bring them to reason, almost like people. Yes, really, there's something human about them, these diseases; if one overestimates them, one's likely to be making a fool of oneself. We have them under control. Take a look at your Hb count: we're able to control this. It'll grumble for quite a while yet, this disease of yours—but it can't get the better of you now. We've got the better of it, and you too, you have.

Me, Christa T. thinks, calmly. Complete honesty, now she knows what that is, too. Knows more certainly than anything that she wants to stay alive, now that she has "come to herself." A command from a realm where the decisions aren't to be doubted. From the same realm, and equally indubitable, came the fear of death as another sort of decision to live, a signal warning her of the greatest danger. Fear coming from constriction. There are nights when one's knowledge of it has deteriorated. I want to live; and I must die. I. Not only can this "I" be lost: it must be. Not any time, after years, decades—never; but soon. Even tomorrow. Now.

Once she spoke about this, in broken phrases, that July evening of our last visit, when I was startled by the change in her, which she called aging, when we swam together and then sat at the round table at lunch. By then she'd been home for weeks, in her new house, and was expecting the baby any day. She can't have been anticipating any repetition of the first nights in the hospital; so she began to talk about them, after we'd strenuously avoided the subject all day. She called the fear not by its name: she said "Shock" and she said "Loneliness"—nicknames, as if there were a taboo, which she acknowledges; and as if "fear" had never been anything but another word for death. She must have discovered that to fight death and to fight fear are one and the same thing. On that July evening she described this state to us, in her broken phrases, as something shocking, unreasonable, and almost disreputable. As undignified and intolerable. She probably admitted to herself, also, that in such cases deception and survival resemble one another closely—deceptively closely. Almost consciously, it seemed to me, she accepted the deception as a means of survival, and lived in it.

There were offers, it's true, prompting her to resign herself to the inevitable. When you've reached thirty, you've got all the really important things behind you—that's what the young doctor says, who always acts very casual, as the enemy's go-between. To make one's own brain an accomplice of the "other side": to accept this offer, a few difficult days and nights—but then one "comes through." The reward for finding, which is always less than the value of the object lost or surrendered.

No, doctor. I know what you mean. But with me it's different. For me the most important things are still to come. What do you think about that?

Whereupon the enemy withdraws his advocate, who changes sides with flying colors. Well now, I didn't mean it seriously, it's just talk. Of course you're right. You'll make it. You'll see, you'll make it all right.

You can even keep the child, Justus says. Don't you see what a good sign that is?

The child? the doctor had said. I'd give a lot to be able to risk operating now.

You'll make it, Justus said. What nonsense. Of course she'll make it.

Then they put her on a stretcher and roll her out of the death room. Every handshake from the nurse a triumph, except that she's exaggerating it rather. I told you we could do wonders. One doesn't want to spoil the nurse's pleasure. She hasn't seen such a glorious wonder done in a long time. The loser waits in vain for the glory to start shining. He feels that wonder and wound are closely related, and actually he's against the idea of anyone being so immoderately joyous at his expense; but he has to realize that now he takes on the responsibility for the smooth functioning of the wonder that's been done.

So the loser is back within reach again. He no longer has any right simply to turn and face the wall, to put on his superior knowing smile as if he alone could distinguish between what is essential and what is not. He has to put behind him quickly his allures; above all, this mistrust, which suggests secret resistance, that must cease. Now he must forget what he, or something in him, had begun to know. With this sort of knowledge one shouldn't mix with people. One puts it behind oneself and one doesn't turn round.

In retrospect one says, perhaps: it was taking me away. Everyone nods, everyone thinks he understands. But nobody knows what she's talking about. You've made it, see? She was apt to look down when they said that. She's ashamed of the experience which sets her apart: the experience which tells you that you can't "make it" or make anything every time.

What's the matter? one can ask her, when weeks later she flings herself, weeping wildly, across the bed.

Nothing. Feel weak.

Ah, she knew it was a pity. She certainly began to respect

herself and to respect also the power that was against her. The one was taking the measure of the other. Born equal. Outcome unsure.

She perused books, looked up the new name they'd given her sickness, and found it. She wrote it down in a letter to me, contrary to her custom: panmyelophthisis. Almost always fatal. But need I talk to you any more about it? Who else . . . It was silly of me to look it up . . .

But gradually the deception overlays the certainty; and we all do our best to nourish the deception in her and in ourselves. And we'd do it again, if deception is another name for hope. Oddly enough, we don't have to believe what we know. Justus confirmed this: he admitted that he'd heard the word "incurable," and then forgot it. One can't live with a stupid, evil, meaningless accident breathing down one's neck.

Christa T. came into her house, into which Justus and the children had moved without her. She put up the curtains, put in cupboards, and began to lay out her vegetable garden.

In the evening, when Justus was out hunting, she often sat alone.

The air would be full of the calls of geese. Sometimes, rarely, she'd write a letter; often she'd read, or listen to music. The moon rose over the lake, she could stand for hours at the window and watch its reflections in the water. The child was moving in her. It happened that she thought calmly about the future, the birth of the child, its life. She knew why, more than with the other children, she wished to see this child in her imagination, to know everything about it. She felt that it was wonderful to be in the world, wonderful that one was in the world. That she could raise her hand to brush her hair back, if she wanted; she felt that was wonderful. To stand in the house, facing the nocturnal lake, just as she had dreamed of it, it was wonderful. Was she dreaming it now? Or did she remember this night, was she remembering it, much later? What had been and what perhaps would never be, merged together and made this night. It was so simple, intelligible, and real. There was nothing to be sorry about, nothing to regret.

She stood and knew that she was remembering herself as nobody else would be able to remember her later. That's how it is, she thought with amazement, it really can be so.

But we'd better be brief.

The child, a girl, was born in the autumn, and was healthy. I think Christa T. had had secret doubts about the child's health, and she was probably relieved. And I think she took it as a pledge, a pledge of life. As a renewal of an old alliance, on which from now on she would again rely. So she regarded it as a breach of faith when she collapsed again.

The look she gave the children, turning back as she sat in the car, might well have been a look of farewell. A repetition of what shouldn't be repeated. Repetition—re-petition . . . The word has a double meaning; one applies to this world, the other to the other. She's calmer this time and asks fewer questions; unasked, they encourage her all the more: You'll make it; they know all about it. Sometimes she takes a long look at the gilded tip of the church spire which she can see from her bed. When it has lasted too long, she reaches quickly for a book. She reads greedily. She resumes her habit of noting statements, lines. The last entry in her notebook is a poem:

> Let this infernal torment stop.
> Once it has been, but here it ends:
> The jostling crush of alien souls
> And distances dividing friends.

At last! she writes in the margin, and this is as much as to say: now there is no death. It's beginning, the thing she so painfully missed: we are beginning to see ourselves. Distinctly she feels that time is on her side, and yet she can't help saying: I was born too soon. For she knows that before long people won't still be dying of this disease.

The medicine seemed to be taking effect; she developed an appetite. She worries about the children being well looked after. She writes in a letter to me: I'd be glad to hear all about your life together, if it's possible now . . .

She realizes that the blood transfusions are becoming more frequent and are lasting longer than the first time. She sees the other, healthy blood dripping from the glass container into her arm; and she thinks: now no power in the world can stop her bone marrow from flooding her own red blood with the destructive white cells. Lived too soon, she perhaps thought; but nobody can really wish to be born and to die in any time but his own. One can wish for oneself nothing but a share in the real joys and real sufferings of one's time. Perhaps that was what she wished for in the end; perhaps she clung to life, to the end, with this wish.

The necessary changes now occur rapidly. She runs a high temperature, has pain. She's given sedatives. When she wakes, Justus is sitting there. She has stopped asking questions; she doesn't mention the children. Quietly and slowly they talk about remote things; and then there's no more talk. She looks at him once more, still recognizes him. But her consciousness is wavering. First the smile disappears from her face, then all expression, except pain. Piece by piece she's withdrawing herself, or something is withdrawing her. Finally, before she stiffens, first of all impassivity, then severity. No more ambiguities; no compromises. Shortly before she dies, she tries to speak. She can't.

She dies early one February morning.

The ground was frozen over, the countryside covered with snow. A path to her grave had to be shoveled clear, and the hole dug with pickaxes. I wasn't there when they put her in. It was summer before I saw the grave. The sandy soil was dry and brittle. The cemetery is in the open country, far from the little town, on a small incline. At the head of the mound two buckthorn bushes were growing. The sky above them was the pure delicate blue that hits one like a blow. And the same again, said Christa T., when you look down at the lake, except that there it's mixed with a little green.

She took off her shoes as the children were doing, while we walked over the hill. She walks barefoot through the rough coarse grass and dangles her sandals by their laces. Now and then she stoops over some blade of grass or other, for her collection of lake-shore flora. She's happy about a thistle. Then we all have to turn around because from here the view opens once more upon the reed-thatched roof of her house. Really suits it, she says, satisfied, it was exactly the right position.

In the night she had a curious dream. In an old building, which I don't know at all, I climb up a staircase, up and up, till I'm right under the roof. Then I come to a big attic, half familiar and half unknown, like the rest of the house. There I find a wall of slats with an opening in it but no door. On the other side of the wall there's a table with brown caps on it, boys' caps: fur, leather. An old man comes, limping. I don't know him but know that he's the school janitor. He says: Next class period they're all going to the exhibition. It occurs to me that behind the wall my old class is sitting. That's why I came here! I'm suddenly glad that I'll be seeing them all again. I remember names. I must have been sick for a long time. I'll wait until the break and then simply go with them to this exhibition, as I used to. —Suddenly I know: I'm not their age any more, I've grown old in the meantime. In an instant the feeling of youth has left me, and I know it's forever. The caps are still lying there, yet I know distinctly that I'm only remembering them. Although I never saw them lying there in those days when I was really young . . . The curious thing was: the pain I felt made me also glad . . .

We sat down in the grass by the unfinished foundations of a small garden house, among the shadows cast by gnarled and disheveled pine trees. The sky, if one looks at it long enough, gradually sinks down over one; only the shouts of the children keep raising it again. The earth's warmth enters us and mixes with our own warmth. Sometimes we talk some more, but not much. We can only guess what we shall have to tell one another later; words, too, have their time and cannot be tugged out of the future according to need. It means much to know they are there.

In two or three hours we'll be saying goodbye. She'll pass into the car a red poppy she has picked on the way to it. It won't last, but you won't mind, will you? No, I don't mind. She'll stay there, standing on the path, waving. Perhaps we'll see one another again, perhaps not. Now we laugh and wave.

Christa T. will be staying there.

One day people will want to know who she was and who it is that's been forgotten. They'll want to see her, and that's only natural. They'll wonder if that other figure really was there, the one we obstinately insist on when we mourn. Then people will have to produce her, create her, for once. So that the doubts may be silenced, so that she may be seen.

When, if not now?